Joey's deep moans cau... transforming into plea... didn't know what the hell she was doing and why she was enjoying it, but she did know she didn't want him to stop. This was just a one-night fling. It didn't mean anything.

Ryan had no plans to stop. He knew what she wanted, what she needed. But he was caught up in a game of cat and mouse. His strokes slowed and he watched with pure delight as she wriggled her rump to urge him on.

"Please," she begged.

"Please what?" He nuzzled her neck and drew the thin flesh in between his teeth.

"Please," she continued, seemingly unable to say much more.

"Is this what you want?" Ryan deepened and quickened his strokes. "Hmm?"

She tried to speak, but no words came.

He slowed down. "I can't hear you."

She bounced her body against his hand, alternating his name with the Almighty. "Yeee... Yes!"

SUPER ROMANCE

ADRIANNE BYRD

When You Were

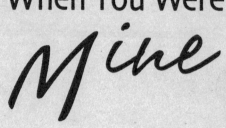

Mine

ARABESQUE®

ISBN-13: 978-1-58314-734-4
ISBN-10:   1-58314-734-9

WHEN YOU WERE MINE

Copyright © 2006 by Adrianne Byrd

www.kimanipress.com

Printed in U.S.A.

This book is dedicated to the one woman who has always believed, instilled hope, shared wisdom and showered me with love: my grandmother— Alice Coleman-Finnley. I hope the angels in heaven know what they're getting into with you.

Chapter 1

For the first time in her life Joseph Henry Adams looked forward to Valentine's Day. This year, Hallmark, 1-800 FLOWERS, and jewelry stores alike were not going to send her spiraling toward a vat of chocolate-chip cookie-dough ice cream. No, sir.

Not only were her prospects of receiving a large heart-shaped box of chocolate good, she was certain a sizable diamond was in the forecast, as well.

"Joey!" Peyton snapped. "Are you even listening to me?"

"What?" Joey blinked out of her reverie and glanced around Cosabellas boutique to her frowning younger sister. "What did you say?"

"I was asking whether you told the girls about your predictions for Valentine's Day?"

"The girls" being the other three sisters: Michael, Frankie and Sheldon—otherwise known as the Nosy Sisters Network.

Joey broke eye contact and glanced guiltily away.

Peyton tsked and shook her head. "You're making a big mistake."

"Don't freak on me, P.J. It's gonna happen. Tuesday night, Laurence is going to drop to one knee and recite a beautiful proposal that's going to make Cupid weep."

"You've been reading too many romance novels."

"And you don't read enough of them. Besides, what's wrong with being in love with love?"

"Nothing." Peyton shrugged, returning a pair of lacy thong underwear to a display table. "I just don't want you to get your hopes up."

"C'mon. I found a credit card receipt for a large purchase from Opulence jewelry store. It has to be an engagement ring," she reasoned confidently. "A nice ring."

Peyton drew a deep breath and offered no further argument.

Joey moved closer to her sister and swung an arm around her slender shoulders. "Trust me. Nothing is going to go wrong."

Film director Ryan Donovan strolled down the red carpet of his latest premier in a shiny penguin suit and with a leggy model on his arm. He puffed heavily on one of his trademark cigars and fought the devil himself to keep his smile leveled at the appropriate angles and his heart pounding at a normal rhythm.

It was times like these when Ryan thought he should have been an actor. Sure, the fans loved him now, but after everyone viewed this latest piece of crap the studio forced him to direct, *Candyland*, they would turn him into mincemeat by morning.

He could hardly wait.

"Mr. Donovan, Mr. Donovan. Who's your lovely date this evening?" A reporter inquired.

"A close personal friend," he lied with a wink, and then prayed the guy wouldn't ask the woman's name. In Hollyweird, glossy pinup girls came off a conveyer belt and required very little assembly to stand prettily and pose for pictures.

He hated interviews and the whole industry knew it. His agent, manager, and even his accountant told him he needed an attitude adjustment, but the truth of the matter was he didn't care whether people liked him— he just wanted them to like and respect his *work*.

Briefly he turned away from the reporters and glanced toward the theater and he groaned. He was at least a mile away from the entrance.

There was nothing like a slow death.

A woman's delighted squeal came a nanosecond before a pair of soft lips were planted against his face. He turned to see his latest pain in the ass and star actress, Carlina Leoni, ham it up for the cameras. Just thinking about the film delays and fines he had to pay because of her melodramatic theatrics was enough to shave a few inches off his plastic smile.

It didn't help matters that at the beginning of filming he and Carlina had gotten a little too close. Too much wine will do that. Add the stress of filming a piece of crap—at least, he was blaming it on stress—and he'd been unable to perform.

Good thing he was beginning to suspect Carlina was a beautiful nut job and that without a doubt Carlina would be the iceberg that sank his once promising career.

Miraculously, Ryan made it down the red carpet and into the theater. His shoulders deflated the moment he was out of camera view, but he was well aware his nightmare was far from over.

Two hours later *Candyland* ended pathetically, with a teary-eyed Carlina glaring into the face of her father's killer and blowing him away Rambo-style. The credits crept onto the screen while an ear-piercing rock 'n' roll soundtrack helped people bolt from their seats.

Twenty-five years in the business and he was now reduced to a joke.

There were a few perfunctory hand claps but mostly people raced toward the door as if a stink bomb had been set off. In a way, one had.

Even his plastic date looked at him as if he'd crawled out from under a rock. Was it too late to go to law school?

During the limo ride home, Ryan was unaware of, and unconcerned with, where his driver dropped off his lady of the evening, though he did remember the look of disappointment on the woman's face when she learned her services wouldn't extend throughout the night.

It was not because he wasn't attracted to the starlet wannabe, it was just that he was still experiencing a little problem…performing in the past few weeks—all right, few months. But as soon as he got his career back on track, his little problem would disappear. He was certain of it.

Much later he arrived at his large neo-style home and

said nothing to the driver as he stepped out of the vehicle and into the chilly night. Tired, he exhaled gloomily as he stared at his sprawling mansion and wondered for the umpteenth time why he needed such a large place.

The answer came in a rush: in his line of work it was more important to appear successful than to actually *be* successful.

As he'd requested, no employees greeted him as he strolled through the glass-and-wrought-iron door. As usual the house's silence was deafening and the cold…humbling.

In the foyer, two sets of arced staircases ascended to the second level of the house. Ryan bounded up the right side, taking two steps at a time. He peeled out of the suit that he would undoubtedly never wear again and headed straight for the shower.

He paid no heed to how hot the water turned or how much the large bathroom filled with thick clouds of steam. He wanted desperately to wash away the grime and the humiliation he'd endured that evening.

No such luck.

Shortly before being boiled alive, Ryan shut off the shower and toweled off. When he opened the door to the adjoining bedroom, a billow of steam preceded him.

Maybe the reviews won't be so bad, he thought dully, but then laughed at how desperately he clung to hope.

Nude, he traipsed across the bedroom's hardwood floor toward the fireplace and started up the gas logs. For a short time afterward he stared into the flickering flames and prayed that tonight hadn't earmarked the end of his career.

Sullenly he turned toward his massive mahogany bed but stopped short at the sight of his reflection in the dresser mirror. At age forty-five he was now the mirror image of his tyrannical father. A man who, in a drunken rage, had busted Ryan's nose, broken a rib and then finally thrown him out of the house.

Ryan held his chin high, his focus zeroing in on the slight crookedness of his nose. Strange, but he drew strength from that facial imperfection—almost like a badge of honor. He had survived that night, even lived through the pain when his mother, as always, sided with his father by simply saying, "You should have known better than to disturb your father when he's drinking."

The problem was that his father was *always* drinking. Something had either happened at his factory job, or he had lost another chunk of change with the boys on poker night, or Ryan was never going to save the family by making it to the NFL on a bum knee. Hell, it could be something as simple as dinner not being ready on time.

He shook his head. That was nearly thirty years ago, and still the painful memories tortured him.

Ryan moved from the mirror and climbed into bed. To his surprise his spirits rose. If he could survive being Clarence Donovan's son then he could survive one bad movie…he hoped.

Chapter 2

"You're dumping me…on Valentine's Day?" Joey thundered wide-eyed.

Dr. Laurence Benson chiseled a thin apologetic smile onto his handsome features as he slid his large, manicured hand across the white-linen-covered table to grasp hers. "I know this may come as a shock, but if you think about it, this is the right decision…for both of us."

Joey twisted her face, unable to comprehend or understand the words flowing from Laurence's mouth. Her only thought was of the receipt she'd found in his coat pocket and the extravagant and romantic evening he had arranged…all just to dump her?

"Jo-Jo, say something," he encouraged with a gentle squeeze to her hand.

She cringed at the nickname he alone insisted on calling her; however, after a time she managed a brave smile. "I don't know what to say," she admitted. "Is there someone else?" There had to be someone else.

Guilt flickered in the handsome doctor's eyes but extinguished before a lie crested his lips. "No."

Joey's body jerked in reaction to the solitary word, and she battled with an instant flare of anger. Yet at his next sentence, the fire fizzled.

"I love you, Jo-Jo. Truth of the matter is I probably always will."

Hope rose in her chest while her free hand sandwiched his. "And I love you, too. Isn't that all that matters?"

"Not always," he said grimly.

Her face scrunched. "You're not making any sense. You love me, so you're letting me go?"

"All right," he huffed, drawing his hand back. "There *is* someone else."

Joey's left eye twitched. Calmly she pressed her fingertips against her temples and stilled the jittery muscle. "What?"

Laurence shifted in his chair and made a cautionary glance around the five-star restaurant. "Look, I know you might be upset, but—"

"Who is she?"

He hesitated, and then his shoulders collapsed. "Does it matter?"

Hell yes, it matters. The twitch returned.

"May I interest you in dessert?" the waitress asked.

"Could you please give us a few more minutes?" Joey inquired, keeping her heated gaze leveled on Laurence.

"Certainly." The waitress moved off.

Joey drew a deep breath and stilled her eye's muscle spasm. This couldn't be happening. She couldn't lose Laurence: the love of her life, the catch of a lifetime.

Her heart fluttered as her gaze slid over him. His handsome face was a sculptor's dream, his skin tone a harmonious blend of honey and caramel, and his body was cut like the finest granite.

Dr. Laurence Benson lived and breathed perfection because he was the very definition.

And he was dumping her?

"Look, Jo-Jo," he said softly. "We never agreed to a monogamous relationship."

Hadn't they? Joey's gaze fell to the long-stemmed roses and huge box of chocolates, but no diamond ring.

Her heart sank.

"You weren't dating anyone else, were you?" he inquired as a slow realization dawned on his features.

"You know I wasn't," she quipped shortly, and then shook off her anger. "Just last week we were talking about houses…and children…about a future together." Joey eased back in her chair and folded her hands.

"And what did we discover? You aspire to be a screenwriter among the A-listers in Hollywood."

"And you're a Beverly Hills cosmetic surgeon."

He studied her with sad eyes. "You want a large family…six children—am I right?"

"You said you liked children."

"I do. I like *other* people's children. I like knowing that after I hold them for about ten seconds they go home."

Stunned, Joey stared at him. Could she give up her dream of children in order to hold on to him? She grew up in family of five girls and a baby brother and she'd always wanted the same for herself. The problem: she was coasting through her midthirties and was well behind schedule.

Laurence leaned forward, and the seductive scent of spice and musk had her longing to curl up against him. "I'm sorry all of this comes as a shock to you, but…we can still be *friends.*"

Joey groaned. That was usually her line.

Sunlight shot through the blinds and sliced across Ryan's head. He sighed and contemplated whether he should bother getting out of bed. Lying there and listening to the stillness was probably going to be the highlight of his day.

However, the silence ended at the sound of footsteps rushing down the hallway. His housekeeper, Guadalupe's, soldier's march.

After a quick rap at the door, the bossy, nosy housekeeper poked her silver head into the bedroom.

"Are you decent?"

Ryan tucked his nude body beneath sheets. "I'm not hungry."

"Always the grouch." Guadalupe's laughter was larger than her husky, five-foot-two frame as she sashayed toward the bed with his breakfast tray. "It's not so bad. You survived."

"Yeah, don't remind me." Ryan groaned as he forced himself to sit up. "What time is it?"

"Time to get up." She placed the tray over his lap. "I have your favorite."

Ryan's gaze dropped to the stack of fluffy buttermilk

pancakes topped with strawberries, surrounded by link sausages and scrambled cheese eggs. His stomach growled and he smiled at his housekeeper.

"Sounds like hunger to me." She winked.

"More like a marriage proposal." He reached for the small pitcher of maple syrup. "You spoil me," he admitted.

"That's my intention." Guadalupe planted her hands on her thick waist. "Every woman knows the way to a man's heart is through his stomach."

"Most women I've gone out with couldn't tell the difference between a skillet and a George Foreman grill." He took his first bite of breakfast and moaned in ecstasy.

"Another satisfied customer."

"Marry me." He shoveled in another mouthful.

She tossed her head back with a hearty laugh. "What would I do with you?"

"Are you kidding?" Ryan teased as he gestured to the room around him. "All this could be yours."

"It's already mine…to clean." She glided back toward the door. "Don't forget you have a two-thirty appointment with Zachary Griffin at Miramax," she reminded him, and then disappeared out of the room.

At the reminder, Ryan set his fork down as his head filled with endless possibilities of how the meeting would go. Would he get the opportunity to direct his dream script, *A Nation's Defense,* or would they push that sappy romantic comedy, *La Bella Vida* on him? Knowing the studio, they would ship him off to Italy before he could say *arrivederci.*

There was nothing about him that screamed romance or comedy. *La Bella* would just be another iceberg sitting in still black water.

Ryan lost his appetite and removed the tray from his lap. After he climbed out of bed, he reached over and opened the top drawer of his nightstand to pull out an old and rumpled screenplay.

It was a damn good script; nearly everyone agreed on that. But was it commercial? Who was the target audience? Lastly and largely, how much was it going to cost?

Getting a project green-lighted was not unlike doing the tango with a starved cougar. Movies were built on favors as well as money. I scratch your back, you scratch mine was the city's fight song. What the hell did talent or telling a damn good story have to do with anything?

So, for the past few years, Ryan did one favor after another. A few paid off, most of them didn't.

But today, by hook or by crook, he had to get his financing.

His gaze dropped once again to the title page and the screenwriter's name. "Joseph Henry Adams, I'll get this film made...somehow."

After a night of crying her eyes out, Joey woke up with a throbbing headache. Even so, she didn't want to climb out of bed long enough to find some aspirins. In fact, she was perfectly willing to spend the rest of her life hidden beneath the folds of her soft comforter.

Closing her eyes again, she sighed when Laurence's congenial smile flashed back at her. Laurence. Sweet Laurence.

"Oh, God. Please say it's not over," she whined.

"Joey?" A voice called out from somewhere in the house.

Dear God. Not now.

"Joey? Are you here?" A second voice inquired.

Groaning, she buried deeper into the bed. In the back of her mind, reason said her efforts were futile, and from the sound of rushing feet, she surmised the whole cavalry had assembled for this attack.

All the saints in heaven couldn't save her from what was coming next.

"Joseph, are you all right?" Sheldon, the eldest and the family's fertile matriarch, placed a comforting hand against Joey's shoulder.

Torn between kicking them out and bawling like a baby, Joey finally chose to just close her eyes and pretend she was invisible.

Of course, her sisters knew all her tricks.

"We're not leaving here until you talk to us," Sheldon persisted.

"I'm fine" was what she wanted to say, but instead a sob blocked her windpipes.

Suddenly the covers were snatched off and Joey was forced to stare at her four concerned sisters through a waterfall of tears.

"Oh, Joey." Frankie, the bejeweled diva, who had the good sense and good fortune to marry a multimillion-aire, fluttered her Harry-Winston-adorned hand across her heart.

"Are you hurt?" Michael asked.

Considering the ache throbbing in her chest, Joey nodded and sat up.

"Oh, sweetheart. What happened?" Peyton asked as the bed dipped from their collective weight.

Stuttering, choking, sobbing, Joey struggled to find

her voice. When she couldn't, she reached for Michael and cradled her face against the crook of her neck and wept.

Michael, the nosiest of them all, tsked under her breath and patted Joey lovingly on the back.

The embrace tightened as more arms encircled her.

It was impossible not to feel the love radiating from her sisters and it was natural for her to want to stay cocooned in their embraces forever. They might be meddlesome, but when it came right down to it, they were Joey's lifelines.

"He didn't propose, did he?" Peyton asked softly.

This time instead of trying to talk, Joey shook her head.

Moans of disappointment surrounded her.

"It's all right," Michael cooed, stroking the back of her head. "There's always Christmas."

Between them, the one sister who undoubtedly understood Joey's plight was Michael. She'd finally made it down the aisle after dating her husband, Phillip, for ten years and being engaged for an additional five. She was an inspiration to any woman who was determined to hang on to her man.

Hang on.

Joey sniffed and eased out of their arms. "I'm okay," she lied. "But...I would love something for my headache."

"I'll get you some aspirin," Sheldon said, and took off for the bathroom's medicine cabinet.

"Do you want to talk about it?" Peyton asked, reaching for her hand.

Joey did...and she didn't. She was new to this kind of emotional breakdown. It was embarrassing how she'd hung her hopes and dreams on a proposal.

Sheldon returned with the requested aspirins and a small Dixie cup of water. "Here you go, sweetie."

Joey quickly popped the pills and quenched her disappointment when it didn't immediately soothe her headache. "I can't believe you guys drove up here to L.A. to check up on me."

Frankie waved her off. "Are you kidding? With Sheldon's heavy foot, it only took three hours."

Up until a year ago, all of the sisters resided in their hometown of San Jose. Joey moved to L.A. first, chasing her dream of becoming a screenwriter and shortly after, Michael and her husband, Phillip, moved there when his job transferred.

"I just don't know what happened." Joey shook her head. "Where did I go wrong?" she finally settled on asking. Her eyes swam. "We were perfect together."

Everyone's concern deepened with their frowns, but they all seemed cautious about pressing her too much.

"He dumped me," Joey confessed, wanting to get over this whole ugly business. "On one of the most romantic nights of my life, he dumps me."

"That bastard." Michael's frown hardened into stone. "I say we go down and put sugar in the tank of his brand-new Mercedes."

"Or key up the paint job," Frankie added.

"Heck, how about we pull that job we did to Peyton's first husband, Ricky? We can break into his place and superglue everything together."

Peyton crossed her arms. "Only, more than half that stuff you guys glued was mine."

"Hey, it was the thought that counts," Michael reasoned defensively.

"No," Joey said, jumping in before they got carried away. "No silly acts of revenge. We're too old for that, don't you think?"

Sheldon crossed her arms over the small bulge of her stomach. "Age is a state of mind."

"Joey's right." Peyton said. "I'm not crawling through any more windows."

The girls' shoulders deflated.

"I just don't get it," Sheldon griped. "He boasted he was crazy about you just this past New Year's."

"I cooked for that man," Frankie added.

Everyone looked at her.

"Well, I supervised," she amended.

"I'm sorry, Joey," Peyton said with commiseration. "But maybe this was for the best."

"The best? How can you say that? He was perfect. *We* were perfect."

The room went silent with her declaration, and Joey looked around confused. "What? You guys liked him. You all said so."

Everyone's eyes couldn't or wouldn't meet her gaze.

"It doesn't matter. I love him and he loves me—he told me so."

"He sure has a strange way of showing it," Peyton quipped.

"Don't start, P.J.," Joey retorted, and smote her with a look of warning. "No male bashing today."

Peyton's wounded look was quickly covered with a broad smile. "Hey, I love men."

The other sisters turned their incredulous gazes toward her.

"Okay. I love *my* man," Peyton amended.

Against her will, Joey's lips curled into a smile. "Exactly, and when you love someone, you should fight for them."

"I thought you were supposed to set them free," Sheldon said. "Isn't that how the song goes?"

Joey untangled herself from her sisters and climbed out of bed. She didn't know where her surge of courage and determination was coming from but a balloon of hope inflated within her.

"I'm not letting Laurence go." She lifted her chin. "He just doesn't know what he wants and probably got scared." She turned and headed toward the closet.

Peyton frowned. "What are you planning to do?"

"I'm going to do whatever it takes to win my man back."

Chapter 3

A nervous Joey twitched at the front door of the Blue Diamond, praying her name would magically appear on the club's guest list. The three times she'd been allowed into the exclusive club was when she was draped on Laurence's arm—mainly because Laurence's brother was the club's owner.

"I'm sorry, Joey, but your name is not on the list." Marcus, the bouncer, a brick building of a man, glanced down at her and shrugged. "I can't let you in."

"C'mon, Marcus." Joey flashed her best smile. She hadn't tweezed, waxed, polished and buffed herself to perfection just so she could be turned away. She didn't even want to think about the damage her first pair of stilettos was doing to her calves right now or how her new bra had her breasts sitting beneath her chin. Tonight, she was a woman on a mission.

"You know me, Marcus. I'm sure it would be okay if you let me in."

"Is this going to take all night?" A woman snapped.

Joey checked her temper and stepped aside.

Marcus scanned the list and then with a wide smile allowed the woman to enter. However, when he returned his attention to Joey, his lips curved downward. "Can't do it. You know the rules."

Joey's heart dropped and tangled with the knots in her stomach. "What's it going to take to get you to look the other way?" she asked with desperation seeping into her voice.

As quick as a whip, a lustful leer sparkled in Marcus's eyes and caught her off guard. Joey fluttered a hand to cover the top of her plunging neckline. She wasn't *that* desperate. "I meant how much money?"

Disappointment blanketed the bouncer's chiseled granite features, but Joey still detected interest.

"What you got?"

Joey snapped open her purse, which was only large enough to hold her ID, a tube of lipstick and a lousy ten-dollar bill.

"You're kidding me, right?" Marcus asked when she slipped the folded bill into his hand.

"C'mon. It's all I have."

"I don't think so." He boldly slipped the money between her breasts. "You know the rules."

Joey slapped his hand away and stabbed him with a narrow glare. Yet, as she turned away, her mind raced with alternative ways to get into the building. Laurence was inside, and she had to talk him out of breaking up with her—with as much dignity as possible, of course.

* * *

"Ryan, my man. You came." Fredrick Benson's loud thunderous voice boomed over the Blue Diamond's bass-thumping music.

Ryan winced as his friend's heavy hand pounded across his back and threatened to dislodge a lung. "A promise is a promise," he chuckled, and drained the rest of his drink.

Freddie, a giant of a man at six foot six, earned the nickname of Cool Freddie for being that—cool. Nothing ever ruffled Freddie's feathers, and he liked nothing more than being the life of the party.

"Well, it's good to see money and fame hasn't changed you." Fredrick took another whack at Ryan's back. "Of course, I can't say the same for my older brother, Larry—cosmetic surgeon to the stars." Freddie shook his head. "Trust me. It's all gone to his head. You should see the number he showed up with here tonight. The girl doesn't have breasts, she has flotation devices."

"I'm guessing they're still great to stare at," Ryan snickered and puffed on his cigar.

"True that. True that," Freddie agreed with a wide, spreading grin. "Are you cool, or should I have one of the girls get you another drink?"

"I'm cool." Ryan cast another glance around the crowded dance floor and placed his empty glass on a passing waitress's tray. "But where's the john? I have a few minutes to kill before Zach gets here."

"More business?"

Ryan cocked a sly grin. "Like Biggie said—"

"More money, more problems," Freddie joined in

and laughed. "The closest set of restrooms is down past the first bar."

."Roger that." Ryan slapped him on the shoulder. "I'll catch up with you later."

"You got it."

Ryan turned and dropped his smile as he navigated through a throng of dancing people. The Blue Diamond, heavy on stylish design, was a sizable night-club, and incorporated three distinct areas into one nighttime destination. The first section was a smoke-free, Asian-inspired lounge with a full bar and an elevated DJ station. Next was the dance floor, Jam, a technological whirlwind of twenty-five flat-screen tele-visions and explosive colors powered by a kinetic lighting system.

The last section was a lush courtyard, which provided an opportunity for an open-air stroll in a Japanese-style garden surrounded by a giant frog pond lined with wooden benches.

However, life in the fast lane no longer impressed Ryan. He'd seen too many people get caught up with the drinking, the women and the drugs. Sure, once upon a time he was footloose and fancy-free, but that was a synonym for being young and stupid.

"Hey, baby. Wanna dance?"

Ryan stalled at the feel of a woman's hand pressed against his arm. He glanced down at the young girl with too much makeup on and was certain she was a few years shy of the club's requirement age of twenty-one.

"I don't think so," Ryan said, and then watched the young lady's gaze drag over him. Undoubtedly the lady's mental calculator tallied in his expensive clothes and tasteful grade of bling-bling.

"Are you sure?" She inched closer, pursing her lips into a perfect pout. "I know how to show you a good time."

He flashed a sly smile. "How old are you?"

"Why? Do you want to be my daddy?"

He glanced at his watch. "You better get home. I think it's way past your curfew."

The girl rolled her eyes. "Asshole."

"So everyone keeps telling me." Ryan turned. At the bar, he extinguished his cigar and plowed ahead. Despite a crowd milling outside the restroom doors, Ryan was relieved to see only one patron inside checking out his reflection in the mirror.

"What's up?" the short Italian asked in a thick accent.

"Nothin'. Just chillin'," Ryan responded, injecting the right amount of street cred into his voice before heading over to a fancy stone waterfall that functioned as a urinal.

"This place is crawling with hot ladies." The Italian popped his collar. "It's impossible for a *brother* not to score in this place."

Ryan snickered and held back from pointing out the truth to the man who was *not* a brother. Instead, he finished his business, zipped up and headed over to the sinks.

The Italian finished obsessing over his hair and gave himself a wink in the mirror. "I'm going in." He turned for the door.

"You get 'em, tiger," Ryan chuckled, squirting soap

into his hand. As he washed up, he practiced his pitch to Zach. "Be firm, be direct, and don't let Miramax talk you into doing some silly romantic comedy in Italy."

Ryan drew a deep breath and stared at his reflection. With any luck, he could make this deal and be home and in bed by midnight.

Tap. Tap.

What is that? He glanced around and frowned.

Tap. Tap.

Ryan's gaze zoomed toward a high bathroom window above one of the stalls. Suddenly it opened and a pair of silver stilettos emerged. Stunned yet amused, Ryan folded his arms to watch. At the sight of long, toned, pecan-colored legs, Ryan's blood stirred.

"Damn it. I'm stuck." The woman grunted, and then wiggled her rump to try to squeeze through.

"And I thought I'd seen everything." Chuckling, Ryan headed toward the pair of gorgeous legs and refrained from touching them to see if they were as soft as they looked; but something else soon caught his attention and he smiled. "Need help?"

The woman stopped wiggling.

"Ma'am?"

"Uh, are you looking up my dress?"

Ryan pulled his gaze away from the lacy white panties and lied, "Of course not."

The woman huffed, wiggled and then after a long pause asked, "Can you please help me? I can't move, and I think I'm losing the feeling in my hip."

Ryan entered the stall and could only think to stand up on the toilet to reach the damsel in distress. Even then, he wasn't sure of what part to grab or hold. He reached and then stopped to contemplate the situation—even wondered if this was some paparazzi setup.

"Can you please hurry? I'd hate to die like this."

"I take it there was something wrong with using the front door?" Ryan settled on placing his hands beneath a part of her butt—a nice, firm butt to be exact—and lifted her upward.

"What are you doing?" the woman yelled.

"Wait, let me just pull—"

"Stop, stop," the woman panted. "You're going to snap me in half!"

Ryan stopped and reassessed the situation.

"I don't think lifting me is going to work."

"You don't say," Ryan griped. "Maybe I should go and get the manager."

"No. No." Panic melded into the woman's voice. "We can do this."

Ryan chuckled. "I take it you're not supposed to be here?"

"Gee. I bet you were the smartest in your class."

Ryan frowned. "You know, I think it's a rule somewhere not to insult the person who's trying to help you."

The woman huffed a frustrated breath. "You're right. I'm sorry."

"Apology accepted." Ryan smiled and again averted his gaze from the woman's Victoria's Secrets. "So what should we do next?"

"I don't know. You have a better view of this."

"A damn good one," he chuckled.

"What?"

"Nothing."

"Why don't I just…"

Before Ryan could react, the woman's sleek legs wrapped around his neck and placed him in a Chinese scissor hold.

"…do this and you lean back and pull me through."

This was one for the record books, Ryan thought. How many men could boast about meeting a woman's crotch before being introduced?

"Okay. Now, pull."

Ryan obliged before there was damage to his air supply, and to his great relief and surprise, the woman's rump cleared the small windowsill. However, a toilet seat wasn't an ideal spot for a game of tug-of-war. Immediately after his great heave, he and the mystery woman were suspended in air for an eternity before their big crash against the linoleum floor.

"Oomph." Every ounce of air flew out of Ryan's body.

"Oh, my God. Are you all right?"

"I think…I'm paralyzed," Ryan croaked beneath a mass of legs and white panties.

The door squeaked open and Jay-Z's rap lyrics bounced off the bathroom's natural acoustics.

"Damn, man," a voice boomed. "Get a room." The door slammed shut behind the patron's dramatic exit.

"Oh, good grief." The woman scrambled off Ryan's chest.

The sudden rush of oxygen to Ryan's brain made him dizzy, and he still had serious reservations about whether he could get off the floor. However, that was nothing compared to the tricks his eyes played on him as he gazed up at the most beautiful woman he'd ever seen. "Hot damn. I've died and gone to heaven."

Chapter 4

"Ryan Donovan?" Joey brushed her hair back from her eyes and then blinked in surprise. "My God. It *is* you." She took his hand and shook it. "I'm such a big fan of your work." She scrambled for her purse, and swore when she glanced inside. "I don't have any of my business cards. Oh, I know." She grabbed an ink pen, took his hand and sprawled her contact information across the palm. "My name is Joey Adams and I'm a screenwriter."

Despite the pain he smiled. "Nice to meet you, Joey."

"What are you doing here?" she gushed.

"Oh, just lying here reminiscing on the days when I could feel the lower part of my body. Good times."

"Ohmigosh. I'm so sorry." Joey scooped an arm beneath his back. "C'mon, let me try and help you up."

"Uh, I don't know if that's such a great idea." However, his words fell on deaf ears as Joey tugged and pulled on his arms. Grudgingly, he sat up before she wrenched his arm out its socket.

"See, you're going to be all right," she panted, propping him against a stall door. "How many fingers am I holding up?"

"What fingers?" Ryan joked with a sly smile and then drank in her beauty. Her wide, warm-chestnut-colored eyes sparkled and he salivated at the sight of her full, kissable lips.

"Are you all right?" Joey studied him. "You didn't crack your skull, did you? Maybe I should go get the manager?"

"No, no. I'm fine." Ryan attempted to stand but was stunned when the room tilted sideways. He reached for Joey as gravity overpowered him; but she proved just as unstable on those high stilts that masqueraded as shoes, and they landed with another splat on the linoleum.

Joey chuckled. "If we keep this up, we're going to break something."

Heat scorched up the column of Ryan's neck and then simmered in his cheeks at the feel of her breasts pressed against his chest. Hell, it was the first time he'd had a hard-on in months.

"Hey, we heard someone was gettin' it on in here," a man announced, bursting through the door with a loud group of rambunctious men behind him.

"Yeah. Can we watch?" another man asked as all eyes fell on Ryan and Joey.

"Sorry, boys, but we're all done," she joked good-naturedly and climbed back to her feet.

More men piled in, trying to steal a peek, and Ryan had to stifle his own disappointment for having their private moment snatched away. When Joey's gaze returned, he smiled and managed to somehow climb back onto his feet.

The shortest man in the crowd, who was also dressed in a hideous pea-green suit, wagged his finger. "Hey, don't I know you?"

Belatedly, Ryan remembered his celebrity status and quickly imagined a barrage of tabloid junkets with his picture and a caption: Famed Director Caught in a Toilet Rendezvous.

"Let's go." Not waiting for a reply, he seized Joey's elbow and guided her toward the door.

"I'm sure I know you," the man continued.

"He does look familiar," someone else said as he passed.

Navigating a path out of the bathroom was like whacking through a sugarcane field, but he managed to get them through without incident.

"Careful. Careful. I don't think these shoes were made for walking," Joey complained.

Against his will, Ryan chuckled. "Then why wear them?"

"Use your imagination," she teased.

Why did you have to say that? Snapshots of Joey draped across his large bed in a fire-engine-red teddy and silver stilettos filled his head and caused his rock-hard erection to ache. Looks like he'd just found the woman to end his little slump.

He slowed down when he reached one of the bars and then turned toward her. "Mind if I ask a silly question, Ms. Adams?"

"Shoot."

"What the hell are you doing breaking into the men's bathroom like that?"

"My name wasn't on the list, and Marcus refused to let me in."

Ryan frowned. "You climbed through the men's bathroom because your name wasn't on the VIP list? Why didn't you just come in through the general admission door?"

Joey stiffened. "What general admission door?"

"Look around," Ryan laughed. "There are hundreds of people here. Surely, you don't think *all* of them are on the VIP list?"

"General admission." Joey closed her eyes as a rush of embarrassment overwhelmed her.

"Ten dollars to get in." He shrugged. "With the place being so huge, its entrance is actually down a block but—"

"Okay, I get it." She shook her head and swore under her breath. "But I still need to get into the VIP section." She started toward the first section of the club. The area would be blocked off with more bouncers and security personnel whose sole jobs were undoubtedly to keep the riff-raff away from "the chosen."

"Why do you *need* to get in VIP?"

Joey sighed. "I have to find someone…and talk him out of making the biggest mistake of his life."

"A boyfriend?"

"Well—sort of." She rolled her eyes. "It's a long story."

His eyes performed a slow drag over her figure. His

body still responded to her every curve. He certainly didn't want to give her up.

"Hey, what about you? You definitely should be on the list. Can you get me in?"

"I'll be glad when we can sleep in our own bed," Lincoln complained to the closed bathroom door, and then mumbled, "I shouldn't feel like some pimply-faced teenager afraid that your father is going to walk in every time I reach for my own wife."

The bathroom door whooshed open as Peyton poked her head into the bedroom.

"What did you say, honey?"

"Nothing." Any hope of making love to his wife died the moment his eyes landed on what appeared to be men's pajamas. "Flannel again?"

"I didn't want you to get any bright ideas while we're across the hall from my father."

"Then let's move to another room. I don't see why we have to stay in Flex's old room anyway. It holds bad memories for me."

Peyton's lips sloped with amusement. The first time Lincoln had ever been to this house, Peyton's family was under the misunderstanding that he was their baby brother, Flex's, new boyfriend. It was in *this* room and while staring at *this* bed that Flex confessed to Lincoln about the lie his family believed.

"C'mon. Don't be that way," Peyton pouted prettily as she approached the bed. "Besides, it's just for one more night."

Lincoln cocked his head and stared at his wife with lazy disbelief. "That's what you said last night."

Peyton leaned in and teased Lincoln with a feathery kiss. "Jamie promised me everything would be ready by tomorrow."

"If not, we're hiring a new decorator."

"Now, don't be like that. Jamie is a good friend of mine."

"If you ask me, that's part of the problem. Never hire your friends because you can never fire them."

"I'm not supposed to sleep with my clients, either," she teased, referring to her dual role as his art agent.

"You're not sleeping with me. That's the problem. C'mon, baby. Don't sleep in your old room. Stay in here with me tonight."

"Lincoln," she warned smiling.

"Please?"

"Don't beg."

He gently pulled her down onto the bed. "Don't you miss me?" Lincoln kissed and nuzzled her neck. He smiled when she sighed. "We can keep it quiet."

"You know I can't be quiet with you," she whispered shakily when his lips traveled across her collarbone.

Lincoln's nimble fingers slid open the top button of her pajamas and another moan escaped Peyton. Just as it was getting good, Lincoln's candy was snatched away.

She climbed off the bed. "See? I'm already getting too loud, and you barely touched me."

"B-but…where are you going?"

"Good night, honey," she sang over her shoulder and escaped out the door before she changed her mind.

"Fine." Lincoln tossed a pillow at the closing door.

* * *

It was past midnight when Flex Adams parked his rented Ford Explorer in the driveway of his childhood home and killed the engine. All the lights were out and he took it as a good sign that everyone was fast asleep.

Sweet success. He had successfully kept a secret from his nosy older sisters and pulled off a surprise visit from Atlanta. Not that it wasn't hard. It was. Damn hard, in fact. Sheldon, Frankie and Michael, in particular, could teach the CIA a few tricks in gathering information.

Climbing out of the SUV, Flex quietly grabbed his luggage and crept to the front door. To his surprise, the lock had been changed.

Flex frowned. He'd had the same key since he was twelve. When did they change it? "Now what?"

He huffed out a breath and glanced around the porch. He moved toward a window and hazarded a glance inside. When he couldn't see anything through the closed blinds, he set his bags down and pulled at the window.

Locked.

He heaved a frustrated breath, but he was determined not to ring the doorbell. Maybe he should go and check all the windows. Stopping to think about it for a moment, he realized he didn't have a choice.

"I didn't come this far to ruin my plans now," he mumbled, and then remembered the great oak in the backyard. How many times had he climbed it after curfew when he was a teenager?

Encouraged, Flex picked up his bags and headed toward the backyard.

* * *

"Please get me into the VIP section." Joey's smile stretched wide across her face as she looped her arm through his.

"You're not going to even attempt to hide the fact you're using me?"

"Me? I would never—well, see this is really important."

"I'm not that nice." He reached into his pocket and withdrew a cigar.

"You're not going to help me?"

"What's in it for me?"

Joey placed a hand on her hip. "How about a warm glow from knowing you helped someone?"

"I did my charity work for the night back in the restroom, remember? I got a sore back for my trouble."

"Sorry about that." Guilt flashed briefly across her face. "So what do you want?"

Ryan stepped forward, his eyes boldly resting on her chest.

Joey placed her hand across her chest. "The answer is no!" Irate, she turned.

Ryan's hands snaked out and latched on to her upper arm. "Okay, okay. You can't blame a man for trying."

She eyed him suspiciously. "You'll get me in?"

Completely smitten and amused, Ryan nodded. "Fine. I'll take you."

"You will?"

"I could say no, especially since I liked watching you squirm and wiggle your rump through the men's bathroom window."

Her face tinted and he took her arm and escorted her toward the VIP section.

Relieved and excited, Joey leaned over and kissed his cheek. She didn't know why she did it, but she was stunned by the crackle of kinetic energy when her lips touched him. She pulled back and stared into his dark-mocha eyes framed by long lashes and felt something flutter in her stomach. She smiled and took another step back and noted how he had the body of a Zulu warrior: tall, broad and strong.

"Are you all right?" he asked.

"Yeah. Fine." She wasn't sure what happened, but she quickly shook it off.

"Well, let's get you into VIP."

Joey sucked in a breath as he slid his arm around her small waist and wondered about her stomach again as he escorted her through dancers, waitresses and security men. Once she made it behind the velvet rope, she scanned the perimeter.

But Laurence found her first.

"Jo-Jo?"

She turned at the familiar voice, her smile wide across her face when she saw Laurence; but then it died when she noticed the tall, silicon-stuffed Italian doll standing at his side. *It can't be.*

Laurence's smile quivered at its edges. "Jo-Jo, what are you doing here?"

"I...I came here looking for you," she managed to say.

The famed actress pressed her body against Laurence and coiled her long arms around his neck. However, it was the diamond ring on the woman's left hand that caught and held Joey's attention.

"Who is she?" Joey asked.

Laurence licked his lips as his gaze skittered to the woman glued to his side.

"I'm Carlina Leoni," the woman answered with a bedeviled smile. "Larry's fiancée."

Chapter 5

Stuck in a looping continuum, Joey stood in the middle of VIP and gaped at Laurence. It wasn't until Ryan reached over and closed her slack jaw that she even had a clue of how ridiculous she looked. Even then she didn't know what to do or say, so instead she spun on her stilts and nearly broke her neck.

Ryan's arms flew out around her waist and saved her from making an even bigger fool out of herself.

"Whoa, sweetheart."

"Jo-Jo, wait," Laurence called.

Ryan's face scrunched at the nickname as he whispered, "You let him call you that?"

"Just get me out of here."

Ryan opened his mouth to protest. The last thing he wanted was to be trapped in some Jerry Springer drama.

"Jo-Jo," Laurence called again and pried away from his true to life blow-up doll and hustled around to block their exit. "Jo-Jo. This is— I'm sorry…but I didn't lie to you. You must believe that."

Joey's hand whipped out and slapped Laurence across the face. The sting in her hand was nothing compared to the pain ripping through her heart. Thoughts of scratching out his eyes and snatching every strand of hair from his *hussy's* perfect head crossed her mind, but remarkably she refrained from turning ghetto.

With his arm still wrapped around her waist, Ryan stepped forward and established himself as protector. For one long heartbeat the men stared at each other.

Laurence glanced around Ryan and stared at Joey. "I thought you weren't dating anyone else?" Accusation laced Laurence's heavy baritone, and Joey was stunned and confused by the flicker of hurt in his dark eyes.

He still loves me.

However, her hopes died when Carlina reappeared and slithered a long tanned arm around Laurence's neck.

"C'mon, *Larry*. Let's dance." Carlina smiled but it seemed aimed at Ryan.

"You hate being called Larry."

Laurence dropped his head and then stepped aside to complete Joey's heartbreak.

Everyone and everything blurred as Joey detached from Ryan and sprinted through the club. "This was a mistake. I can't believe… Oh, God." She placed a hand over her stomach. "I think I'm going to be sick." She trekked through the club in record speed, heedless of the people she bumped into or nearly bowled over.

"Joey, wait up," Ryan called.

"Why didn't I listen to Peyton or Michael or Frankie?"

"Joey!"

Bursting through the glass doors, Joey collided into Marcus's back.

The bouncer turned and then blinked in astonishment. "Hey! How did you...?"

She sprinted around the large man.

"Joey, will you *please* slow down?" Ryan caught up with her. "Where are you going?"

"Home." She stopped to jab her hands against her hips. "Where in the hell did I park my car?" Exasperated tears leaked from her eyes.

Ryan settled his hands onto her shoulders and forced Joey to make eye contact. "Look. You're upset. Why don't you let me drive you home?"

Her lips curled as she attempted to pull herself together. "I appreciate that, Mr. Donovan." She sniffed. "Truly, I do...but it's not necessary. I'm fine," she lied.

Ryan frowned. "You don't look fine...and please call me Ryan." He gave her shoulders a gentle squeeze. "I'm not sure what just happened in there...but I'm worried about you," he admitted.

"Don't." Joey shrugged off his hands. "I'm a big girl. Nothing happened that a tub of ice cream wouldn't fix. I'll either cry myself to sleep or pass out from an extreme sugar high," she laughed, but her voice cracked.

"Joey—"

"Oh, there's my car." She stepped around him and backhanded her tears. Her body trembled as she clung to what little dignity she had left. Not only did she make a fool of herself, but this time she managed to do it in front of a big-time director.

Ryan's hands fell to his sides as he pulled himself upright and followed close behind.

Neither spoke during the short time it took to reach her old silver BMW and fumble for her keys. When she opened her car door, she turned back to face Ryan with a wobbly smile. "Thanks…for everything."

Tenderly he wiped the tears she'd missed from her face. "I'm sorry we couldn't have met under happier circumstances."

"Yeah…well…"

"Maybe we can hook up again…to discuss your scripts?" he offered.

"Really?" She sniffed, scared to believe that something good was going to come out of this.

"Really." He reached inside of his pocket and handed her a business card.

"I'd love that. You still have my information?"

He flashed her the palm of his hand. "Got it right here."

His warm smile buffered the rain pouring down inside of her.

"Good night," he whispered and leaned forward and planted his lips against hers.

Joey sucked in a startled gasp but failed to react because her thoughts muddled together and her heartbeat pounded in her ears. He tasted like charm, sophistication and danger all rolled up in one. He was as addictive as chocolate.

Ryan's body went haywire. She tasted wonderful and felt like a dream. Hot damn, he was definitely back in the game. Overconfident, he pulled her closer and glided his hands down her backside.

Joey jumped back and swung.

Stars rained before his eyes. He chuckled, but had a devil of a time blinking the stardust away. "Wow. That's quite a punch you have there."

"Asshole." She threw his business card at him and then slid in behind the wheel.

"Look, I'm sorry. I couldn't help myself." He continued to laugh. "Why don't we go back to my place and talk about it over a drink?"

She slammed her door, started up the car and backed out of her parking space without sparing Ryan another glance.

"Is that a no?" he shouted after her. His gaze followed the car until it disappeared. He huffed and turned back toward the club. "I guess the slump continues."

Lincoln held his breath as he crept down the hall in search of his wife's childhood bedroom. He'd lain in bed, staring up at the ceiling for as long as he could, yearning to hold his wife until he thought he would go insane. He was a grown man with *needs* and he had a gorgeous wife just three doors down who knew how to satisfy those needs.

At last he arrived at his destination. Excitement rushed through him, and a smile ballooned across his face as his hand landed on the doorknob. Lincoln cringed as the hinges creaked in protest. Once he had sufficient space, he inched into the room and cringed again when he closed the door.

Success was well within Lincoln's grasp as he padded over to the whitewashed canopy bed. He could almost feel a pair of devil horns spike through his head as he slid beneath the sheets next to his wife. Hard and aching, Lincoln curled into a spoon behind his wife's firm buttocks. "Baby?" he whispered against her ear.

"What are you doing?" Peyton's silky voice floated back toward him.

"What does it feel like?" He planted kisses down the column of her neck.

"It feels like you're doing *exactly* what I told you *not* to do."

"C'mon. Don't you miss me?" He slid his hands beneath her hideous flannel pajama top. "Don't you miss this?"

Peyton chuckled softly. "That's not the point." She rolled around to face him, but before she could chastise him, he kissed her.

"Tell me I can stay," he commanded lovingly. "Tell me you want me to make love to you."

She moaned as his large hand cupped her firm breast.

"I'll take that…as a yes." He chuckled and then returned to business.

Flex vowed to go on a diet.

He'd always been a big guy, a muscular guy, but there'd been a time when he could climb the oak tree in his childhood backyard in twenty seconds flat. Tonight, however, he suffered through three near wipeouts, a potential hernia and a possible slipped disc…and he was only halfway up the damn tree.

If any of his firefighter buddies saw him now, he would never hear the end of it. Had an extra twenty pounds reduced him to this?

Flex swung out his hand for another branch, and then his foot slipped off the limb below him before he made contact.

Good ol' reliable gravity paid a visit and slammed him against the earth. He opened his mouth to scream…but his body forgot what to do with oxygen— completely understandable since pain seized every muscle, nerve and sensory gland.

He blinked and two fat teardrops pooled and slid from the corners of his eyes just as his lungs kicked back into gear and sucked in their first drag of oxygen.

"Ouch," he whimpered.

For a while, he remained content to lie flat on his back, staring up into the night sky. Really, what harm would it be to spend the night outside?

Thunder rumbled and a few drops of rain splattered against Flex's face.

"Lord, you have to be kidding me."

Thunder rolled and lightning temporarily lit the sky.

"Okay, okay. I'm going. I'm going." Locating a source of reserve energy, Flex sat up and ignored the pain in his lower back.

Maybe I should check all the windows again.

He liked that idea. What business did a grown man have climbing trees anyway?

Flex limped around the house again as rain fell in light, thin sheets. But by the time he turned away from the last locked window, he was in the midst of a torrent.

Just go ring the damn bell.

Tempted, he turned to go do just that but then stopped. *I'm not a quitter.*

Flex drew a breath, squared his shoulders and returned to the oak tree. Determination, more than skill or grace, propelled his six-foot-four frame skyward.

A second before he reached for the window, a horrible thought occurred to him. What if this window is locked, too?

He grumbled under his breath at that possibility, yet a wave of relief washed over him when the window opened.

Yeess!

There was more straining and grunting involved in actually getting through the window. Once inside, triumph roared through his veins...but then pain brought him back down to earth again.

Flex glanced longingly at the comfort his old bed offered. Lord, how much he wanted to dive in and sleep for a full week; however, he still had to sneak downstairs and lug up his suitcases.

Frustrated, annoyed, and flat-out grumpy, Flex crept out of his bedroom door and tried his best to tiptoe through the house's still darkness.

Peyton jerked away from her husband's passionate kiss. "What was that?"

"What was what?" Lincoln asked dumbfounded, and then dismissed the question and tried to recapture his wife's lips.

She turned her face away. "Didn't you hear something?"

"Just music, bells and all that romantic crap. Now, where were we?" He hiked her left leg higher on his hip.

"What if it's Daddy?"

"I'm your daddy right now," Lincoln chuckled.

She smacked his hard chest. "I'm being serious."

Exasperated, Lincoln sighed. "Do you want me to go check it out?"

"Do you mind?"

"Actually—"

Peyton rewarded him with another smack. "I told you this was a bad idea. Go back and sleep in the other room."

"Whoa. Whoa. I was just kidding. Of course I'll go check it out. If it's all clear, we'll pick up where we left off. Agreed?"

"Just go check it out," she hissed, and pushed at him to hurry.

Flex retrieved his suitcases and closed the front door. Gone was the excitement of surprising his family. Judging by the pain in his back, he needed to be more concerned with whether he needed a trip to the hospital's emergency room.

He stopped at the base of the stairs and set his luggage down. A couple of Tylenol should do the trick, he concluded, thinking about the economy-size bottle his father usually kept in the kitchen.

Feeling around the dark living room, Flex bumped into furniture his sisters had the habit of rearranging whenever their moods struck them. He'd almost made it through the challenging labyrinth when his arm bumped something and he jerked around to catch it. Instead, he kicked another mysterious object, which tipped over and landed solidly on his big toe.

"Goddamn it!"

Lincoln froze on the center of the staircase with his ears perked. *Someone is in here.*

Adrenaline pumped hard and steady through his veins as his brain quickly tried to apply reason. In fact, it was probably just his father-in-law on the prowl for a late-night snack.

Not probably—most likely.

"Marlin?" Lincoln descended cautiously down the stairs. However, the last stair was booby-trapped with bags of some kind, and Lincoln quickly found himself flat on his back with stars dancing before his eyes.

"Who's there?"

Lincoln frowned at the familiar voice and winced through the pain as he struggled to sit up. "Francis?"

Chapter 6

Again cocooned in the Blue Diamond, Ryan proceeded back to VIP. The loud music barely penetrated his troubled thoughts, while his body mourned the loss of a woman he didn't know and most likely would never see again.

"Ryan, my man. Where have you been?" Freddie pounded his heavy hand against Ryan's back. "I've been looking all over the place for you. Zach is waiting, man."

"Damn," Ryan muttered under his breath. "I'd forgotten about Zach. Where is he?"

"Sitting in VIP." Freddie hooked his arm around Ryan's neck. "Don't worry. I draped a few girls on his arms and kept him liquored up." Freddie winked. "I doubt he noticed you were MIA."

"Thanks, Freddie. I owe you one."

"Really? 'Cuz I got this cousin who's been trying to break into the business…"

His attention shifted from his friend's rambling and focused on the man he spotted out of the corner of his eyes.

Larry.

The man was still entangled with Carlina Leoni, aka his career iceberg, and appeared to be undaunted by what had transpired between him and Joey.

"Excuse me, Freddie." Ryan maneuvered through the crowd with his eyes locked onto his target.

"Hey, Ryan. Where you going?" Freddie called out.

Ryan stopped behind Larry and tapped him on the shoulder. When the tall stranger turned, Ryan's gaze and then his fist zoomed across the man's perfect square chin.

Larry crashed against the floor and then looked up stunned. "What the hell did you do that for?"

"That's for Joey." Ryan shook his hand to relieve the pain.

Carlina gasped, although belatedly, and then dropped down beside her fiancé. "Baby, are you all right?"

Ryan turned and ignored the wide eyes of spectators.

"Whoa. Whoa. Whoa." Freddie slid to a stop next to Ryan. "What's going on here?"

"That jerk just punched me," Larry barked, glaring up at the men. "I want him thrown out of here."

Ryan's eyes flew to Freddie. For the first time he took in the men's resemblance. "Is *this* your brother?"

"Unfortunately."

Larry struggled back to his feet and made a great show of dusting himself off. "If you're not going to handle this, then maybe Mr. Big-Time Director would like to take this outside and finish what he started."

Remarkably, Carlina just smiled.

Ryan stepped forward, welcoming the challenge.

"Oh, pipe down." Freddie grasped Ryan by the elbow. "I'll handle this." He tugged at his friend.

Ryan refused to budge.

"Let it go," Freddie said coolly, and this time managed to lead Ryan away.

"You throwing me out?" Ryan inquired.

"Hell, no." Freddie chuckled. "I'm buying you a drink."

Flex clicked on a light and frowned down at his brother-in-law. "Linc, what in the hell are you doing here?"

Grunting, Lincoln sat up. "I was just about to ask you the same thing." He held up a hand. "Can I get a little help here?"

Despite his pain, Flex grabbed hold of Lincoln's hand and assisted him.

"I came down here because Peyton thought she heard something and insisted I check it out. Since it's just you, I'm going back to bed." He reached over and patted Flex on the back. "Good night."

Flex restrained Lincoln by the shoulder. "Don't tell P.J. I'm here. I want to surprise everyone in the morning."

"Not clogging around here like some giant oaf you're not." Lincoln chuckled. "You're about as quiet as a space shuttle launch."

"Very funny." Flex snatched up his bags. "You and P.J. aren't exactly quiet church mice." He rolled his eyes and hitched his voice to mimic Peyton's lusty moans. "Oh, big daddy. Oh, big daddy."

Lincoln chuckled.

A soft gasp drew the men's attention. Both looked up to the top of the staircase to see a stunned, and clearly embarrassed, Peyton wrapped in her robe. Without saying a word, she turned on her heels and marched down the hall.

"Nice going," Lincoln mumbled under his breath, and then raced up the stairs. "Baby?"

So much for his surprise. Flex's shoulders slumped before he proceeded up the stairs.

"C'mon, baby. Open the door," Lincoln begged.

"Good luck," Flex whispered as he passed by in the hall, but he was unable to prevent the smile on his face from reflecting in his voice.

Lincoln ignored him. "I'm sorry, honey. I know it wasn't funny."

Flex reentered his old bedroom and placed his luggage at the foot of the bed. Once he withdrew a pair of pajama pants, he made a beeline to his adjoining bathroom and turned on the shower.

The hot, soothing spray of the water immediately performed wonders in erasing the aches and pains from his sore limbs. As he lathered up, his mind drifted to how happy he was to be home—crazy sisters and all.

He sobered for a moment and wondered if his fall knocked a screw loose. Undoubtedly the next ten days would be filled with inquiries about his love life—detailed inquiries. However, he had nothing to report.

Nada. Zilch. Nothing.

Flex sighed and dipped his head low beneath the

spray. If his sisters thought it was hard for them to meet a good man, they should check out how difficult it was for a *man* to meet a good man.

Shaking his head, he shut off the water. If he told his sisters he wasn't dating anyone, he would give them less than thirty seconds to start suggesting friends or a friend of a friend as possible partner material.

Well, I could lie and say I was dating someone....

Nah, he'd already been down that road—and ended up with a new brother-in-law.

Shoving his thoughts to the back of his mind, Flex stepped out of the shower, toweled off and slid on his pajamas. When he finally returned to his bedroom, he was stunned to see Lincoln climbing in beneath the sheets.

"Did I miss something?"

Lincoln punched his pillow and dropped his head back. "You have the couch."

"Excuse me?" Flex tossed his towel to land on his suitcase. "This is *my* room."

"Correction. It *was* your room. Tonight it's *my* room—especially since you got me evicted from Peyton's bed."

"Don't you two have a house somewhere?"

"Renovations." Lincoln reached over and tossed a pillow to Lincoln. "The couch."

"I don't think so." Flex tossed the pillow back and smacked his brother-in-law in the face. "I didn't just endure airport hell and nearly kill myself climbing that damn tree in the backyard just so I can sleep on the couch." He stormed toward the bed and peeled back the sheets on the vacant side.

"What are you doing?"

"Going to bed. You're more than welcome to sleep

on that side, but I'll be damned if I'm sleeping down-stairs." He clapped his hands and the lights went out.

Lincoln clapped the lights back on. "We can't share a bed."

"I'm not moving." Flex yawned, clapped and closed his eyes. "And make sure you stay on that side of the bed—*big daddy.*"

Joey wanted a drink, a gun and a priest—in that order; instead, she settled for a carton of cookie dough ice cream and a pair of scissors. The moment the first scoop entered her mouth, euphoria coursed through every inch of her body. By the time the cool dessert glided down her throat, the feeling vanished and she shoveled more and more into her mouth, trying to get it back.

During short breaks, she proceeded to cut up every picture she could find of Laurence. For a time, she took immense pleasure slicing his face in half, into quarters, and then smaller and smaller. After a while even that simple satisfaction waned.

She returned to her ice cream as more tears arrived. Before long she was a sobbing, gooey mess. It didn't help that her mind conspired against her. Every time she shoved one image of Laurence out of her mind, a thousand more crammed inside.

How on earth did I mess this up?

She sat still in the center of her bed, dressed in her SpongeBob SquarePants pajamas, and waited for an answer. Instead all that came was an image of that creep director shoving his tongue down her throat. She should have bitten it off.

"It's not fair," she mumbled against her spoon. "Why

can't I find true love?" She sniffed and mopped her face with the back of her hand. "Even Peyton has been married twice."

There has to be something wrong...with me.

Joey nodded at her conclusion and forced herself to climb out of bed. Shuffling across the cold wooden floor, she stopped in front of the full-length mirror and dragged her gaze over her reflection.

Her depression sank lower.

Sure she had curves, but certainly not like the Coca Cola bottle curves Laurence's new fiancée sported. Sitting her half carton of ice cream down on the floor, Joey stood tall and lifted her B-cup breasts and frowned. If more than a handful was a waste, why did men flock to the Ds and double-Ds of the world?

Joey cocked her head from side to side.

"I could always get implants," she whispered and turned to the side to see if she could imagine herself stuffed to the max with silicone.

Next her gaze traveled to her thin lips. She had always hated they weren't as full as Peyton's or Frankie's, but now her sugar high had her considering injecting collagen into them.

Joey squinted at her face. Were those bags under her eyes? When had she developed those?

She frowned and then noticed how the act caused her forehead to crease with lines. Botox could fix those. Her critical eyes then roamed over her thick mane. Before this moment, it had been one of her favorite features. Now she found fault with the heavy, straight mass.

Laurence, once again, popped into her head. Had he noticed all her flaws?

Joey rolled her eyes. Of course, he noticed. He was a cosmetic surgeon for Pete's sake. He made his living perfecting women…and Carlina looked as though she had just rolled off the showroom floor.

Suddenly, it all made sense.

Laurence couldn't marry anyone who wasn't perfect—and she was far from it. She sniffed while her self-esteem plummeted. However, as time ticked by and the ice cream depleted, Joey's depression morphed into anger. From there, revenge seeped into her mind.

She smiled wickedly. When it came to revenge, there was only one sister to call. Joey shuffled over to the nightstand and picked up the phone. "Hello, Michael?"

Chapter 7

Ryan had a sinking feeling he was going to Italy.

"Lake Como and Milan, Italy," Zach said. "Paradise."

Ryan refused to be pacified and grunted into his drink. Moviemaking was his life. Movie politics were his worst nightmare.

Zach laughed, gliding his hand through his prematurely graying locks as his Irish green eyes flashed. "Aw, c'mon. Don't look like that. Have you ever been there? The sun, the land—the women." He jiggled his eyebrows. *"Le molto belle donne."*

Ryan's brows squeezed together. "Is there a language you *don't* know?"

"Never cared for Portuguese."

Their waitress appeared, showing more skin than

clothes. "Can I get you fellows anything else to drink? Boss says everything is on the house." Her gaze locked with Ryan's as she smiled. "We all heard how you decked his up-tight brother." She inched closer to him. "Is there any way *I* can thank you, as well?"

Ryan didn't mistake her offer and smiled. However, his body responded as if he'd been splashed with freezing-cold water. "No. I'm good."

"Then I'll check with you later." She winked and sauntered off.

"What the hell is wrong with you?" Zach questioned. "Did you not check out the ass on that girl? It brought a damn tear to my eye."

"Don't let Maggie hear you talking like that," Ryan warned.

"Come, now." Zach placed a hand over his heart. "I'm a happily married man. There's a difference in looking and *doing,* if you know what I mean."

"If you say so." Ryan thought about all of Zach's lusty leers, club hopping and lap dances and just didn't understand the terms of his friend's marriage.

"But what about you? You're forty-five years old. When are you going to find a nice girl and settle down?" Zach asked.

"Me?" Ryan laughed.

"Yeah, you." A glint of seriousness reflected in his eyes. "Don't tell me that you still don't believe in holy matrimony."

Ryan reached for another cigar. "Regardless of what most people think around here, Hollywood and marriage do not mix."

"I know, I know," Zach droned. "It's hard as hell

trying to wade through ambitious actresses and gold diggers, but sometimes, man, you just have to take a leap of faith. You know what I mean?"

He nodded absently and reminisced on a beautiful pair of long, toned legs gliding through a bathroom window. A smile curled his lips.

"Maybe you *have* found the right girl." Zach grabbed his drink and leaned forward. "Who is she?"

Ryan blinked out of his reverie to notice the Cheshire grin on his friend's face. "I didn't say I met someone."

"You didn't have to." Zach snickered. "The look on your face says it all. Is she an actress?"

"There's no Mrs. Right, but I had a good candidate for Mrs. Right Now that I let slip through my fingers," Ryan said, unable to wipe the grin off his face.

"Ah, who is she?" Zach glanced around.

Ryan clammed up and puffed on his cigar.

"Hey, I thought we were friends?"

"So did I." Ryan's annoyance returned. "The studio promised to green light *A Nation's Defense* if I directed *Candyland.*"

Zach winced. "Yeah. That was a stinker."

"I told you that, when I read the script," Ryan said. "And every day while viewing dailies."

Zach shrugged as his lips sloped unevenly. "Hindsight is always twenty-twenty."

That was Zach's answer to everything and it pissed Ryan off how his good *friend* was trying to pull the old bait-and-switch maneuver on him.

"C'mon." Zach sobered at Ryan's permanent frown. "I know what you're thinking and you're wrong. I'm trying to get your finance package together, but you know how *slow* things work in this town."

"I'm only aware of how fast my career is tanking. My first film was nominated for three Golden Globes and now, twenty years later, I'm begging for scraps. What the hell happened?"

"It's just a slump. Don't worry about it. Trust me. I'm going to take care of you."

Ryan envisioned a nail slamming into his coffin. "If I had a nickel every time I heard that, I would have my financing."

"Very funny."

Ryan held up his glass and signaled to the waitress for another drink and then caught sight of the smudge of ink on his hand.

"Oh, no. No, no."

"What's wrong?"

He set his drink down and stared at his hand. Just great. Now he had no way to contact Joey—not that she wanted to hear from him.

"Ryan?"

"Uh, nothing." He waved for the waitress again.

"C'mon. Relax. Have another drink, pick out one of these delectable beauties and let me worry about the money."

Famous last words.

Zach leaned forward. "Now back to your love life. This girl you were smiling about, she's not one of Rachelle's escort girls, is she?"

"What?"

"Well, that was Kitten you took to the *Candyland* premier the other night, right?"

"I didn't retain the name." He frowned at his friend. "How do you know her?"

"How do you think? She's an—"

"Actress," Ryan cut in.

"Now, I'm not saying there's something wrong with Rachelle's ladies, but word is…you're not exactly using all the fringe benefits her girls offer."

"How in the hell do you know that?" Ryan thundered.

Zach laughed. "Rachelle is infamous in this town. Nice girl from the Bible belt. Never was a good actress, though her skills on the casting couch are legendary. In the end, she's starred in, like over a hundred films."

"Madame Rachelle is Rachelle Tanner?" Ryan asked, stunned.

"Ah, you heard of her." Zach took a deep gulp of his drink.

He most certainly had. And though he never used "the casting couch," the practice was alive and well. When Ryan finished marveling over this latest tidbit, he noted Zach still waited for an answer.

"My love life is fine. Thank you for your concern."

"Just hit a dry spell, eh?"

Ryan shifted again. "Something like that. I should cut out of here."

"So soon?"

He glanced at his watch and stood. "It's 3:00 a.m."

"Exactly. It's still early."

Ryan shook his head. "I think it's time you went home to tuck in your wife." He winked. "I'll see you in Italy."

"You won't regret it." Zach also stood. "Who knows?

Once you peek at what Italy has to offer, you might come back home a married man."

"I highly doubt that."

"Never say never."

"Larry, I'm waiting," Carlina called seductively from her posh pink bedroom.

Dr. Laurence Benson cupped another hand of cold water from the bathroom sink and splashed it against his face. In the end, it failed to temper his anger or soothe the pain of his throbbing jaw.

That's for Joey.

Who was the famed director to Joey? As the question floated in his mind, he wondered why the hell he cared. Pausing, he examined his jaw and could see it swelling.

"Laarrrry," Carlina sing-songed.

"I'm coming." He turned from the mirror and cut off the bathroom light. When he strolled into the nauseatingly pink bedroom, he stopped to see his fiancée posed over plush pillows and dressed in a lacy pink peignoir.

"I hope you like cotton candy."

A small smile tugged at the corners of his lips, but he found the sex kitten didn't successfully erase Joey Adams from his mind.

What in the hell was wrong with him? Was it possible that he'd made a mistake?

"What's the matter?" Carlina sat up with a pout.

"Nothing…I just need to make a phone call."

She blinked. "Now?"

He nodded absently and dug his cell phone out of his pants pocket. "Yeah, I'll go in the living room to make the call."

"But—"

"It will only take a minute," he said, and strolled out of the room.

Michael showed up at Joey's front door dressed in black…which included the silk cap and combat boots. "Let's rock and roll."

Joey, still dressed in her pajamas, blinked numbly at her.

Michael jabbed a hand into her hip. "Don't tell me you changed your mind about this?"

"No…yes." Joey slumped against the door. "I don't know."

"I do." Michael stormed into the house. "This man played you, and he's not going to get away with it. So wipe your face and get dressed. SpongeBob isn't going to cut it."

Michael's bossiness sprang Joey into action as she acquiesced with a quick nod and rushed to her room. Fifteen minutes later she was dressed and sitting in the passenger seat of Michael's Volvo.

"There's a thin line between love and hate," Michael said with her eyes locked on the road ahead. "Some of these men would do best to remember that."

Joey nodded. "Do we have a plan?"

"I always have a plan." Michael turned onto the freeway. "Dr. Laurence Benson will rue the day he crossed an Adams."

Glancing over at her sister, Joey wondered for the first time whether Michael was really referring to Joey's ex-almost-fiancé or someone a little closer to home. "Mike, is everything okay between you and Phil?"

Her sister clenched her jaw. "Peachy."

It was a lie, Joey realized as she studied her. "Do you want to talk about it?"

"No." Michael took her exit ramp without a turning signal and Joey quickly rechecked the security of her seat belt. "Maybe Peyton was right. We are getting too old for toilet papering front yards."

"I agree." Mike took another sharp right.

"You do?"

"Yep." Mike glanced over at her. "I have something better in mind."

Joey's stomach clenched with anxiety. Michael's calmness worried her. What exactly had she gotten herself into?

She didn't have to wait long for an answer.

Michael, an artist when it came to revenge, had packed for a masterpiece. Laurence's high-tech security system seemed to insult Michael's intelligence, and they were in the house in less than a minute flat. Once inside, they started off with a Michael classic: super gluing everything in place.

Next, they poured industrial strength blue dye in the hot tub, filtered Nair into all the shampoo bottles, and squeezed liquid soap onto his toothbrush. In the kitchen, they punched holes into the cans of tuna and then hid them in different cabinets for a 360-degree stank effect.

In the garage, since the Mercedes was gone, they poured three bottles of baby powder into the defroster vents of Laurence's Porsche and then turned the knob so it was set on high defrost for whenever he started the car. Joey wished they had cameras so she could see Laurence's reaction when he came home.

It was official: Joey had gone over to the dark side.

Michael took great pleasure in brushing a thin coat of vegetable oil inside and outside of the windshield and for a final touch: rocks in the hubcaps.

"Now, let this be a lesson to you, sis. Never lose your cool, never let them see you cry and never let them get the best of you."

Joey nodded, but her curiosity about the state of Mike and Phil's relationship bubbled to the forefront of her mind.

By the time they returned to the Volvo parked two blocks away, Joey grudgingly admitted she felt much better…right up until she saw the blue lights flashing behind them.

Chapter 8

The morning sun warmed Lincoln's face as he snuggled closer against Peyton, dreading the prospect of having to get out of bed. Hands down, last night was the best sleep he'd had since the renovation began on their new home.

A lazy smile drifted across his face as his mind crowded with erotic images of his wife. He had no trouble recalling the taste of her sweet lips or the silkiness of her thighs. In fact, he wanted to bury himself between them right now.

He squeezed her tighter, drew her back against him, and placed a tender kiss against her lower earlobe.

"Lincoln?"

"Hmm?" he moaned.

"Did you just kiss me?"

He chuckled softly, squeezed her close. But before he could answer, the heavy baritone penetrated his mind's purple haze and his eyes widened with a jolt.

"Linc?"

"Uh…" Lincoln took in his surroundings. To his horror, it wasn't Peyton he snuggled against but instead his mountain of a brother-in-law.

"Lincoln, why did you just kiss me?"

"Why are you holding my hand?"

A solitary knock against the door drew the men's attention, but it opened before either had a chance to react.

"Linc…" Peyton glided through the door and froze. "What—"

"Is anyone coming down for breakfast?" Marlin Adams, the family patriarch inquired as he, too, stepped into the room and then stood shell-shocked next to his youngest daughter.

"Hi, Dad." Flex smiled. "Surprise."

The color drained from Marlin's face.

Lincoln finally found his voice. "This isn't what it looks like."

Peyton and her father remained silent and rooted in place.

"See what had happened was—"

"He kissed me," Flex said, and consequently made matters worse.

Peyton's eyes shifted to her husband. "You kissed my brother?"

"I…I thought he was you," Lincoln offered as an explanation, but could tell by the rise of her eyebrows she found that hard to believe. "Well, I know he doesn't *look* like you, but…I told him to sleep on the couch."

"I need a drink." Marlin turned on his heel and marched out the way he came.

"It's eight o'clock in the morning," Peyton reminded him.

"Good point. I better make it a double."

Lincoln detangled himself. "Mr. Adams, I swear nothing happened." He turned toward Flex. "Tell him."

Flex smiled and folded his arms behind his head. "Aw, he'll be fine."

Embarrassment blazed up Lincoln's neck. "Mr. Adams!"

Peyton covered a hand over her mouth in a sad attempt to muffle a snicker.

"I'm so happy you find this amusing." Lincoln jumped out of bed. "This is *your* fault."

"Mine?" Peyton laughed. "I didn't tell you to put the moves on my baby brother. I knew you were horny, but—"

"Don't you dare finish that sentence," he warned, grabbing his robe and rushing out the door. "Mr. Adams! Wait. I need to talk to you!"

Peyton turned her wide grin toward her brother. "Welcome home."

"It's good to be home."

The two collapsed with laughter.

Joey pried open her wet, swollen eyes only to stare blankly at the ceiling. For a moment last night's crime spree seemed like a bad dream, but when the unmistakable sound of steel slamming on steel echoed around the stone walls, the truth hit home. It had been no dream.

Neither was their arrest.

"We're entitled to a phone call," Michael barked to a passing guard. "Both of us!"

"Yeah, yeah, yeah," the guard chanted. "You'll get your call. Just hold on to your panties."

Michael exhaled a long huff. "Can you believe this crap?" she asked Joey.

"I can't believe a lot of things right now," Joey sighed and sat up on the metal bed. Her gaze swept to the small cluster of women in the opposite corner. All of them dressed in rubber-band skirts, too-tight tank tops and ridiculous high heels. However, one had on a pair of familiar stilettos.

"I can't believe you didn't shut off the alarm," she whispered toward her sister.

"I did shut off the alarm." Michael shrugged. "I just didn't shut off the second alarm—the silent one."

Joey rolled her eyes and somehow remained calm.

"I want my phone call," Michael yelled.

"The more noise you keep up, the longer it takes to get your call," Ms. Stilettos informed them in between smacks of her bubble gum.

Michael's shoulders slumped. "Thanks for the tip."

"Well," Joey sighed. "If we go to jail, at least we'll be there together."

Michael's gaze cut toward her. "That jerk won't send us to jail." A ripple of doubt crossed her hard expression. "Will he?"

"I don't know what *Larry* will do," Joey answered. The dregs of her sugar high ebbed away and in its place a maddening headache pulsed. "Are you going to call Phil?"

Michael's hands tightened around the cell's bars. "I don't know. Then again, San Jose is five hours away—three if Sheldon drives. That's a long time to wait for another family member to get up here."

Joey cocked her head and stared at her sister's granite pose. "Mike, what's really going on with you and Phil?"

Her sister didn't answer.

"You know *I* can keep a secret."

For a long while Michael said nothing, but then when she finally spoke, it was just above a whisper. "Phil and I—"

"Michael Anthony Matthews and Joseph Henry Adams?" the female guard shouted down the jail's long corridor.

Michael wiped her eyes. "Over here!"

"Michael and Joseph? What are you two—drag queens or something?" Ms. Stilettos asked, approaching Michael and inspecting her face. "You *girls* are the best I've ever seen."

Joey rolled her eyes.

"You two ladies are in luck. Dr. Benson called from the airport and stated he wasn't going to press charges."

The other women in the jail cell clapped and whistled.

"Those two were beginning to sound like a soap opera," one of them griped.

Michael flashed them a bird.

Joey ignored them. "Did you say the airport? Is he going out of town?"

"What do I look like, honey—his personal secretary?" The plump guard sauntered into view as she inserted the key into their jail cell. "All I can tell you is that you're free to go."

Ryan couldn't believe he paid someone five times a week to torture his body into shape. It was insane and a necessity. The world was a young man's playground, more so today than any other time, and he was in it to win.

During his ten-mile run, Ryan thought a great deal about Joey. In particular, her long legs and her mischievous-but-innocent dark eyes.

Maybe when he returned from location, he could call an agency or something to find her. He knew her name and he definitely remembered every detail of her face. Was six months sufficient time for a woman to mourn a breakup? If he called too soon he could accidentally be filed into the rebound-guy category, or was it called the transition guy? He never mastered relationship lingo.

Of course, there was the small problem of her hating his guts, but he would cross that bridge when he came to it.

"Good workout," his trainer, Ken, boasted as they slowed to a stop at Ryan's front door.

Ryan nodded and bent low at the waist to drag in a deep gulp of air. He glanced at Ken, annoyed the man didn't have sweat glands.

"How long are you going to be gone this time?"

"Four to six months."

"Long time." Ken smiled. "Do you need me to come and help you keep your regime up?"

Hell, no. "Let me get back to you on that."

"Sure thing." Ken jogged over to his Mercedes with

way too much reserved energy. "I'll make sure my people call your people," he joked.

"You got it." Ryan forced a smile and pretended to be amused. "Catch you later." He pushed open his door and entered the house.

"You have a package," Guadalupe announced, appearing out of nowhere and handing him a FedEx envelope.

Ryan frowned as he accepted it. "Morning to you, too."

"Sorry." She smiled. "Good morning. Breakfast is ready." She floated toward the kitchen. "One more day," she sang.

Curious, he followed. "What's with the big grin?"

Her lips widened. "Don't you remember what tomorrow is?"

Ryan quickly sensed a trap. "Monday?"

"Sí." She marched back over to him and pinched his cheeks. "It is also the night you and my cousin, Maria, are attending that roast for Sydney Poitier." She touched her forehead and crossed her heart. "That man is still hot." She cleared her throat. "They call me Mr. Tibbs." She giggled at her bad impersonation.

"Is that tomorrow?" His heart dropped—not because he had to attend the roast, but because he had to escort his housekeeper's permanently inebriated cousin.

"Oh, don't worry." Guadalupe patted his arm. "She promised to be on her best behavior."

Ryan's brain assessed the excuse file; but before he could rattle one of them off, she waved a finger at him.

"No excuses." Her eyes flashed. "You said if you were in town and weren't dating anyone, you would take her. So, you'll take her."

He clenched his teeth and forced on a smile. "I didn't say anything."

"Good. It's settled." She patted his arm again and turned. "Besides, you need a wife."

"I said I would take her out—not marry her."

"One can lead to the other," she sang happily. "You're having French toast this morning."

Ryan ripped opened his FedEx package and withdrew an airline ticket. When he read the date, relief bubbled within him. "Aw. Sorry, Guadalupe, but it looks like there's been a change of plans."

She faced him as her eyes narrowed. "What sort of change?"

"Film production is starting early." He held up his ticket. "I leave for Milan first thing in the morning."

Silence entombed Michael's car as the sisters rode back to Joey's apartment. Gone was any taste of revenge from last night's shenanigans. Only despair and loss resided in Joey's heart now.

"I'm going to write a new screenplay," Joey announced. "Artists create their best work during depression—Hemmingway, Picasso, Beethoven."

"None of those were screenwriters."

"Hell, have you seen the crap that's been coming out in the theaters lately? They're all products of Prozac and Zoloft cocktails."

"If you feel that way about it, why don't you get out of the biz and just do The Great American Novel or something? You've been at this screenwriting thing for years."

Joey shrugged and stared gloomily out of the window. "That's not such a bad idea." Her thoughts traveled back to Ryan Donovan. Was he really interested in reading some of her work…or was it just another Hollywood line?

Minutes later Michael pulled to a stop outside Joey's apartment. "Here you are, kid." She turned in her seat. "Why don't we keep what happened last night between us?"

"Mum's the word." Joey laughed and opened the car door. "You know, we never did finish our last conversation."

Her sister feigned ignorance, but Joey saw through the charade. "Well, when you're ready to talk…"

"Misery loves company?"

"Something like that."

Michael nodded. "I'll get back to you on that."

Joey hesitated and then cocked her head. "Is that a promise?"

"Yeah." Michael's thin smile looked more like a flat line. "It's a promise."

Joey nodded though she remained dubious as she climbed out of the car. The moment she closed the door, Michael pulled away. After the car faded from view, Joey turned toward her apartment. It was no wonder Michael didn't want to discuss Joey's woes with her—her own love life was the toilet.

Shuffling into the apartment, Joey couldn't wait to dive into bed. She didn't want to think about Laurence, screenwriting, or jail—especially jail—ever again. After locking the front door, Joey turned and spotted the flashing red light on her answering machine.

She hit the play button.

You have one new message.

Joey rolled her eyes at the decline of her popularity and kicked off her boots.

"Hello, Jo-Jo. It's Laurence…"

Chapter 9

Joey reached for the couch and steadied herself at the sound of Laurence's voice. By the way her knees trembled, she quickly realized she needed to sit down.

"Joey, are you there? Pick up." Laurence's deep exhalation floated over the recorder. "I, uh…oh, hell. I don't really know where to begin—other than tonight when I saw you…I don't know."

She inched closer to the phone and strained to hear every nuance of his voice.

"I'm confused," he admitted. "I thought I'd made the right decision…but now I'm not so sure. I mean, this is crazy, I leave for Milan tomorrow and…" He sighed. "I think…I still having feelings for you…I mean I still *love* you and—"

"Laarrry."

Joey jerked and frowned at the familiar purr on the line.

"I'm coming," Laurence's muffled voice called back, but then it turned crystal clear when he spoke back into the mouthpiece. "Look, Joey. I better go." There was a long pause before he added, "Bye."

End of new messages.

Joey sank deeper into the couch in stunned silence. She shook her head as hope rose in the center of her chest. He loved her. He said so.

What about his fiancée?

A smile crept across her face. He's having second thoughts. She wasn't out of the game yet. Joey jumped to her feet, but she halted short of dancing a jig.

"Milan?" A wave of panic seized her. He'd called the police station from the airport. "I have to go to Italy."

"Adams residence." Peyton answered the kitchen wall unit as she entered the kitchen. "Oh. Hi, Phil. How's it going?" Her eyes swept over to the kitchen table where her husband huddled close to her father.

"Mike?" Peyton frowned and gave the conversation her full attention. "No. Michael is not here. Did she say she was coming down?"

Phil hedged, but concern filled his voice when he spoke again. "Uh, no. She didn't say where she was going actually. We, uh, sort of had a little fight yesterday."

Peyton turned her back toward the table and lowered her voice. "Is everything okay?"

"Sure, it was just a little disagreement." He coughed. "No big deal."

She didn't believe him.

"I'm sure she'll turn up any moment now," he added.

"But if she does show up down there, will you tell her to give me a call?"

"Sure. No problem." Peyton held the line, waiting to see if he'd add anything.

"Okay, then I guess I'll catch you later?"

"All right. Take care of yourself." She waited.

"You, too." He hung up.

The dial tone immediately hummed in her ear and she returned the hand unit to its cradle.

"Who was that?" her father asked, looking up from his bowl of Grapenuts.

"Phil." Peyton replayed the conversation in her mind and still believed something was terribly wrong.

"What did he want?" he asked, watching her.

Not wanting to sound any alarms, Peyton shrugged to downplay her suspicions. "Nothing. He was just looking for Mike. She might be on her way down."

Marlin nodded. "Probably caught wind that her brother was down here." He chuckled. "I wouldn't be surprised if she had this house bugged."

"You must be talking about Michael," Flex said, entering the kitchen with a wide smile and a slow gait.

Marlin shifted in his chair while Lincoln glared at his brother-in-law.

"What happened to you?" Peyton asked. "You look like you're in pain."

In the same methodical motion, he retrieved a bowl and a box of Grapenuts. "I had a little incident with Mr. Oak in the backyard."

"What kind of incident?"

"Well, I sort of fell out of it." He opened the fridge and grabbed the milk.

"You hauled your big butt up that tree?" Lincoln quaked with laughter. "Now, that would be something I'd like to see."

"Trust me. It couldn't have come close to seeing you two in bed," Peyton retaliated on her brother's behalf.

"Or the look on your face when you kissed me this morning," Flex added.

"You kissed him?" Peyton and Marlin thundered in wide-eyed shock.

Lincoln shrunk six inches right before their eyes. "I told you I thought he was Peyton."

"First I'm not even going to tell you how much that hurts my self-esteem or my self-image, but how far did you go before realizing he wasn't me?"

Lincoln opened his mouth.

"Wait!" Marlin held up his hands and then pushed back his bowl of cereal. "I don't want to hear this."

"Nothing happened!" Lincoln protested to a dubious looking audience. "I swear."

The front door slammed and caught everyone's attention.

"Where is he?" Frankie and Sheldon sang. They rushed inside and then screamed when their eyes landed on their baby brother.

"Oh, I can't believe it. You're actually here," Frankie exclaimed, planting kisses all over his face. "Why didn't you tell us you were coming? We could have planned a party."

"You just answered your own question." Flex winced while being pulled from one sister to the other. He went on with his usual pretense of hating the attention, but in truth he loved it.

"You know Mike is going to have a fit when she gets here," Sheldon warned, repositioning her two-seat stroller. "She takes pride in organizing everyone's life. Whether they want her to or not." She rubbed at her belly. "Oh, if this child don't get off my bladder."

"Trouble with baby number five?" Peyton asked, leaning over the stroller to coo at her niece and nephew.

"Just the usual rigmarole. You'd think that I would be used to this."

"You should take a breather," Frankie said, pulling a chair from the dining room into the kitchen. "You know, take a vacation from mass reproducing."

"She'll do no such thing," Marlin piped up, scooting up from the chair and then plucking his grandson from the stroller. "Did you forget your mother and I had six children back to back?"

Sheldon and Lincoln beamed.

Frankie and Peyton rolled their eyes.

And Flex simply shrugged.

"That's what I thought." Marlin harrumphed and returned his attention back to his grandson.

"So!" Frankie said to Flex. "Are you seeing anyone new?"

"Just my husband," Peyton chuckled.

"Peyton!" Lincoln colored. "That's not funny!"

"Did I miss something?" Frankie asked.

"Yeah. Whatever it is, it sounds pretty good." Sheldon's gaze bounced around the table.

"It's nothing." Lincoln shot his wife and brother-in-law a lethal glare of warning.

Frankie leaned over and planted a comforting hand

against Lincoln's shoulder. "When are you going to learn? *Nothing* stays a secret in this family?"

Before Lincoln could protest any further, Peyton brought the two sisters up to speed on this morning's shenanigans.

"I swear, I thought he was Peyton," Lincoln protested.

Peyton jabbed her hands against her hips. "You keep saying that like it's a compliment or something."

Lincoln tried to respond but only managed to open and close his mouth.

Flex enjoyed ribbing Linc and was relieved the subject and focus had been shifted from him.

"So, Flex. You didn't answer my question. Who are you dating now?"

Frankie turned her dark, smiling eyes toward him. His luck ran out. "I, uh…" He glanced around the room to see all eyes on him—including his father. He cleared his throat. "I'm single at the moment."

"Fabulous!" Frankie clapped her hands. "My hairdresser is a wonderful man and I've been telling him all about you."

Flex drew a deep breath and rolled his eyes.

"Wait, wait." Sheldon held up a finger. "I have the perfect man for him."

Peyton laid a comforting hand against Flex's shoulder. It wasn't really necessary. He'd prepared for this moment ever since he'd decided to come home. And he would likely have to go through it all over again once he traveled up to L.A. to visit Joey and Michael.

"Actually," Lincoln cleared his throat and drew everyone's attention. "I know someone."

The kitchen fell silent.

"You know someone for what?" Flex asked cautiously.

Lincoln's face reddened as he shifted in his chair. "I, sort of, told a friend, er…this dude about you."

The room went silent again for a spell, and then Frankie laughed. "Let me get this straight. *You* found a date for Francis?"

Lincoln continued to darken as he nodded.

Sheldon joined her sister laughing, then Peyton and then Marlin.

"Well, Lincoln," Frankie said, admiringly. "You are now an honorary member of The Nosy Sisters' Network."

"Hear, hear!" Peyton and Sheldon exclaimed.

Flex slumped back in his chair. "Great. That's all I needed—another *sister.*"

First thing Monday morning, Joey bolted into Rodeo Drive Cosmetics Surgery Center. As always, the moment she entered the spacious and elegant center she felt like a wart on an extremely large nose.

She rushed down the long, polished wooden floor toward the reception area, hoping the bright fluorescent lights didn't highlight her flaws to all the waiting patients sitting in the lobby.

Suddenly she thrust up her B-cups and held her chin high. Fake it until you make it, right?

"Hello, Ms. Adams." Heidi Olson, another Laurence Benson creation, flashed her powder-blue eyes and fluttered a tight smile. "What can I do for you?"

Joey wasn't fooled. Heidi couldn't stand her guts— and the feeling was mutual.

"I was hoping to get some information." Joey

stretched her lips wide and hoped it resembled a smile. She would like to say the young woman's brows lifted at her statement, but it seemed her morning Botox shot had her brows permanent stretched in the center of her forehead.

"What sort of information?"

"I need to know the name of the hotel Dr. Benson is to be staying at in Milan?"

"You mean the hotel that he and his fiancée will be staying at?"

Humiliation blazed up Joey's body and scorched the apples of her cheeks. Did the whole office know? "Can you please just tell me the name of the hotel?"

"Sorry." Heidi shrugged her shoulders and blinked at her prettily. "That's confidential information. I can't help you. But I could make you an appointment—say, perhaps breast augmentation?"

"No need. Breasts were meant to be biodegradable."

"Or you can use them to attract yourself a good husband...say a rich doctor even. Maybe you should ask Carlina Leoni?"

"Or maybe you can kiss my naturally tanned ass."

"Ladies, what is going on up here?" Dr. Beverly Bryce hissed under her breath. Her green eyes flashed at both of them in disappointment. "We have patients."

Joey liked Beverly. She was a beautiful redhead who could give Nicole Kidman a run for her money.

"Well?" Beverly asked.

Joey swallowed her pride. "I need the name of the hotel that Laurence is staying at in Milan."

Beverly lifted her chin and then motioned for Joey to follow her.

Joey glanced at Heidi and gave her a sour smile.

"I shouldn't be doing this," Beverly said, closing her office door behind Joey. "Dr. Benson would probably kill me if he found out I gave you this information."

"My lips are sealed," Joey said anxiously, and pretended to zip her mouth.

Dr. Bryce's eyes twinkled. "All right. He's staying at the Hotel Principe di Savoia Milano."

Joey leaped and enveloped Beverly in a brief hug. "Thanks. I can't tell you how much this means to me."

Beverly pulled back and smiled. "Good luck. I'm rooting for you."

Chapter 10

"I'd like a ticket to Milan, Italy." Joey struggled to still the wild pounding of her heart as she handed the Continental agent her passport and anxiously tapped her fingernails.

"When will you be returning, Ms. Adams?"

"When?" She blinked.

"Yes, ma'am."

"Uh, I'm not sure." How long will it take to win Laurence back? "I better make it a one-way ticket… for now."

"Yes, ma'am." The agent returned his attention to the computer, where he typed enough keystrokes for a novel. "Our first available leaves in thirty minutes. I believe I can get you a seat on that one." He peered back up at her.

"Perfect." Joey tempered her excitement and kept her fingers crossed.

He typed some more. "The only seat available is in first class. Will that be okay?"

"Sure."

After a few menial questions, the agent looked up with a smile. "All right. That will be $2,644."

She blinked and then reached into her purse to hand over the credit card her sister gave her for emergencies. This was sort of an emergency. Joey's lips fluttered with a weak smile.

When the agent swiped the card, a wave of fear rippled through her. How was she going to pay Frankie back? She didn't have that kind of money.

"Here you go, Ms. Adams." The agent handed back her card, passport and then shortly after handed over her ticket. "Your flight leaves out of terminal six, gate sixty-five. We hope you enjoy your flight."

With the first part of her mission accomplished, Joey flashed the man a bright smile. "Thanks. I'm sure I will."

In the next minute she cursed the ticket agent for failing to mention that terminal six was located in the next state. Racing to her plane was like the Olympic tryouts. When the gate came into view, she spotted an attendant closing the door.

"Wait! I'm coming! I'm coming!" She flailed out her arms and made a spectacle of herself, but she did manage to stop them.

"You just made it," the gate attendant joked and took her ticket.

"Yeah, lucky me," Joey panted.

The woman's smile widened. "Enjoy your flight."

Joey rushed through the door and waited to breathe a sigh of relief until she sat in her seat.

She headed down the aisle while the pilot rattled off about their expected arrival time in Italy.

"Sixteen hours?" Joey's head snapped up when she realized what the captain said.

"We're getting ready for take-off," a stewardess stated from behind. "Ma'am, can I help you find your seat?"

Joey turned toward the platinum blonde with brunette roots. "I got it." She smiled and then returned to reading the numbers above the seats. When she located 8A, she was pleased to see it was a window seat, and then groaned when she recognized the man seating in 8B.

"Oh, dear God."

The famous director pulled his eyes from his cluttered papers and met her gaze. "Joey?" He blinked in surprise.

She huffed and rolled her eyes. "So far this trip is off to a bad start."

"Ma'am?" the stewardess nudged.

"Oh, let me help you." Ryan unfastened his seat belt and helped Joey place her carry-on luggage in the overhead compartment.

"What's the price of helping me this time—or are you going to shove your tongue down my throat again?"

"Is that a question or a request?" He winked. "Aisle or window?"

She waved her ticket stub. "Window."

Ryan swept out his arm. "After you."

She shook her head and took her seat.

"I know that fragrance," he said, thoughtfully. "Pleasures, right?"

"Yeah. Estée Lauder." Joey eyed him as she strapped on her seatbelt. "Should I be worried or concerned you know so much about female perfumes?"

"A little bit of both, I think." He settled back into his seat. "So this is what you look like in regular clothes." He gestured to her simple jeans and T-shirt attire. "I like it."

"I'm glad it meets your approval," she said cheekily, and then realized she was flirting and composed herself. She took a deep breath as the plane pulled away from the gate.

Flying had never been on Joey's list of favorite things. She endured it for business or pleasure from time to time, but it usually involved her sweating a lot of bullets and downing several minibottles of liquor.

"Are you all right?" Ryan questioned.

"Huh? Oh, yeah." She released the death grip on her chair and forced a smile. "I'm fine."

The plane taxied toward the runway, and Joey's farcical smile collapsed in on itself and she began to singing "Somewhere over the Rainbow." Now, if only she could carry a tune.

Amusement colored Ryan's face as he folded his arms. "I take it you don't like flying?"

"Uh, I don't mind it," she lied.

The plane jerked, and Joey unsuccessfully stifled a scream.

Ryan's head rocked back as laughter burst from his chest. "You are a lousy liar."

"Fine. I lied. I hate flying." She shrugged. "It's no big deal."

The engines revved and Joey's entire body tensed and the death grip on the chair returned. "'Somewhere over the rainbow…'"

Ryan studied her, while the plane raced down the runway.

"Oh, why am I doing this?" she whined, and slammed her eyes shut.

"You know what always helps me at times like these?" he asked in a conspiratorial whisper.

Joey peeled open one eye. "What?"

"I imagine making love to a beautiful woman." A crooked grin sloped his face. "Say, for instance…right now, I'm picturing you draped in something soft and lacy. Oh, let's not forget those sexy stilettos." He jiggled his groomed eyebrows.

"You're what?" Joey thundered. Embarrassment and shock fused and scorched her neck, cheeks and ears.

"Oh, c'mon. It's easy." He leaned closer. "You give it a try. Just picture you and me lying naked on the beach."

The plane lifted off the ground.

"I will do no such thing!" She pushed him back toward his seat. "I don't know you." How could she have been so wrong about him?

"I don't know you, either. What does that have to do with anything?" He grinned.

The plane steadily climbed higher.

"It has everything to do with everything," she argued while her eye twitched. "Don't think that just because you're some big-shot director I should be flattered by indecent proposals."

"I didn't propose anything." He shrugged but held on to his smile. "I just suggested that you use your imagination."

He leaned over once again and this time she leaned back to avoid his touch.

"Ah, what a beautiful view. Don't you think?"

Joey turned and glanced out the window, stunned to see they now glided smoothly through the cerulean-blue sky.

A soft bell dinged overhead.

"Ladies and gentlemen, I have turned off the seat belt light. You are free to move about the plane."

"That's my cue to visit the little boy's room. Excuse me, won't you?" He winked, unfastened his seat belt and bolted out of his chair.

Joey pulled her stunned and confused look from the window to watch him as he made a beeline to the restroom. Did he purposely distract her with that garbage about imagining her naked?

Her gaze shifted back to the window. It's possible. Joey relaxed and felt silly. The other night Mr. Donovan had started off being a gentleman. The stunt he just pulled did help get her mind off take-off and it was funny—not unlike something one of her sisters would have done.

Besides that, Mr. Donovan was a serious Hollywood player. Sitting next to him for sixteen hours should be like a dream come true. If only she had a few of her scripts on hand to pitch to him. Then again, he probably hated people constantly pitching movie ideas to him at inopportune times.

When Ryan finally returned to his seat, Joey met him with a bright smile.

"Looks like someone's mood has improved." He withdrew the stack of papers he'd stashed in the aisle seat. "Does this mean you gave my little exercise a try?"

"No." Her lips widened. "But I do want to ask you something."

"Shoot." He removed a pair of glasses from his shirt pocket and slipped them on.

Joey paused and admired how distinguished the glasses made him. Why hasn't this man made *People*'s most beautiful list? "That stuff you said back there—" she cleared her throat "—did you mean it?"

"Back where?" he asked nonchalantly, and kept his gaze focused on his paperwork.

"Back at take-off," she persisted. "Were you making all that stuff up about—" she glanced around and lowered her voice "—picturing me naked?"

He chuckled. "What's the big deal? I'm sure I'm not the first man to do so."

She blinked, dumbfounded.

Ryan glanced out the side of his frames, and another rumble of laughter tumbled from him. "My. My. My. You're certainly a different woman from the one I met climbing through the men's bathroom window the other night. Don't tell me you're a prude when it comes to nudity and, dare I say, sex?"

"I most certainly am not. I love sex," she thundered, and then reddened when she drew curious looks from surrounding passengers. She flashed everyone a nervous smile and wished that she could shrivel up and disappear.

"Well, I don't know about the rest of the passengers," he whispered. "But I'm happy to hear you love sex.

Then again, you know what they say about people who brag too much?"

Joey frowned.

"That they're the ones who aren't getting any," he answered his own question.

"You really are an asshole."

"You keep saying that." He winked and returned to his paperwork.

"It's because it's true." Joey rolled her eyes. She had to endure sixteen hours of this? She would rather become a contestant on *Fear Factor*. How dare he even suggest that she was a prude! She was considered the footloose and fancy-free sister in the family.

She shifted in her seat and continued the argument in her head. Now, lately, she hadn't been her normal club-hopping self, but that was because Laurence was more of a homebody. A night on the town for him was attending the charity of the month with a bunch of doctors who all hinted at the famous faces they worked on.

She frowned. If that was true, why had Laurence been at the Blue Diamond with Carlina Leoni—his fiancée? Joey shook her head and continued to mope. Carlina, a woman born into money and prestige, leapfrogged to fame when a sex tape of her and some heavy-metal star was stolen and sold over a gazillion copies over the Internet. Joey wasn't *that* footloose and fancy-free.

"Okay. So I might not be the most experienced woman in the world," she mumbled aloud. "But I am still going to will my man back."

Ryan lowered his papers and studied her. "Are you talking about the same man you bitch-slapped in front of thousands of people?"

She shifted in her seat again. "I was upset."

"So I gathered." He folded his arms and warred whether to confess that he'd also stuck up for her honor and decked the guy when she'd left. "Tell me. Do you and this Larry character do this often?"

"Do what?"

"Break up, get back together, break up and get back together? Is this a game you two play so one day you can be on one of those crazy talk shows?"

"No, of course not. We're very much in love." Joey drew a deep breath. "I just need to remind him of that—that's all." Ryan's chuckling crept under her skin. "What is so funny?"

"If you don't know, I'm not about to tell you." He shook his head. Was this the woman he'd considered calling when he returned to California? She was not the brightest bulb on the marquee, or the sharpest tool in the toolbox, or—

"I know what your problem is," Joey's snide voice interrupted his assessment.

"And what is *my* problem?"

"You've never been in love."

He responded with more laughter.

"Whatever. I know I'm right." Joey turned and stared out at the clouds. How could she have ever thought this man was a gentleman?

"I'm sorry," he said.

Joey crossed her arms and refused to look at him.

"But you are wrong. I've been in love. Many, many times, in fact."

That declaration caught her attention, but she remained dubious. "I'm not talking about lust, Mr. Donovan."

"Okay. So that takes about fifty people off the list. But it still leaves me with quite a list."

"Fifty people?" Joey inched away as if he was contagious. "Just how many people have you been with?"

He smiled and his dimples winked at her. "I didn't sleep with all of them or even half of them. I was just in love with them—sometimes in silence."

"Okay. I'll bite. Name one."

"Adenika Towns." Ryan rested his head back on his seat while his eyes turned dreamy. "She was a beautiful goddess with smooth coal-black skin and with eyes so dark they looked like polished onyx. She always wore the finest dresses, and she had the thickest, longest pigtails in the schoolyard."

It was Joey's turn to laugh. "All right. You had me going for a minute."

"Love is love. And I loved me some Adenika."

She drew a deep breath, but could feel the corners of her mouth twitch upward.

"Is that a smile I see?"

Her lips ballooned wide. In that instant she allowed her gaze to take in his deep dimples, his thousand-watt smile and his glossy black eyes. Damn, he was good-looking.

"And for the record—yes. I made it up." He winked.

Joey blinked in confusion.

"At take-off," he reminded her. "I don't know much about you, but I do know that you can't sing."

She laughed and relaxed, but when her gaze lowered to his hands, his fingers were crossed. She laughed. "You're funny."

He grinned and adjusted his spectacles. "Don't tell anybody."

Charmed, Joey laughed again and stole another glance at the handsome man sitting beside her. *Maybe the flight wouldn't be so bad after all.*

Ryan cleared his throat. "Now back to you *loving* sex."

Then again...

Chapter 11

Ten hours into their sixteen-hour flight, most of the passengers in first class had reclined their seats and rested their heads on small, borrowed pillows. There were a few light snorers and a couple of full-throttled bulldozers who sounded as if they were slicing the plane in half.

Only Ryan and Joey's overhead light remained on while they huddled together and exchanged stories.

"So it was love at first sight with you and *Larry?*" Ryan inquired, not bothering to veil his sarcasm.

"Not exactly," Joey plunged ahead, either ignoring or not picking up on his tone. "The stars were just lined up correctly. I'm the right age, he meets all my qualifications—"

"What?"

Joey blinked. "What, what?"

"Whatever happened to flowery prose or poetry? Things like 'I knew we were meant for each other the moment his hand touched mine' or 'the first time we kissed a bolt of lightning shattered my world and I knew I could never live without him?' Isn't that the kind of crap women eat up?"

"Sure—in books and movies—which I love. But in real life, you need a little more science and a check list."

His frustration mounted as he struggled to keep up with the conversation. "What's so scientific about the stars being aligned?"

"I don't know. My psychic can explain things a little better than I can."

Oh, yeah. She fits into Hollyweird quite nicely.

"I know what you're thinking." Joey smiled. "I'm not crazy. Well, maybe crazy in love." She giggled.

Ryan rolled his eyes.

"Look, love is worth fighting for and that's all I'm doing."

He could end this conversation, but his amusement grew with every word she uttered. She thought that she was a soldier for love. He believed she was crazy—in a cute, amusing sort of way.

"So what's your plan?" he asked, injecting a fake nonchalance into his voice. Again her big, beautiful brown eyes blinked at him.

"Plan?"

Ryan braided his fingers in his lap and then twirled his thumbs. It was hard not to be enchanted by her innocent, slash naïve, slash ditzy personality. "You do have a plan to win Dr. Benson back." He smiled. "Your last one didn't work out so well."

Joey's shoulders dipped as her confidence evaporated from her face. "Granted I wasn't prepared for the fiancée bombshell and—wait. Did I tell you he was a doctor?"

"No…but it turns out I'm pretty good friend's with his brother."

"Ah, Cool Freddie." She nods. "I met him once. Don't think he cared for me."

"I find that hard to believe," he said without thought. She frowned. "Why?"

"Well…" Ryan took the question as permission for his gaze to openly caress her face and figure. "You're a very attractive woman. Beautiful, in fact."

Her brows furrowed. "That's pouring it on a little thick."

Was she for real or was she fishing for another compliment? He needed to shift the conversation back to the subject at hand. "I'm still waiting to hear what your plan is."

Again Joey drew a deep breath. "I'm going to talk to him," she announced.

Ryan waited for her to elaborate, but she turned her attention to the window. He couldn't help but ask, "Is that it? You're just going to talk to him?"

"Yes," she said calmly and braided her fingers together. "He told me yesterday morning that he loved me."

Ryan's brows shot up as he crossed his arms. "Did he, now?"

"Yes. Well…at least he said so on my answering machine."

"Uh-huh. And you believed him?"

Joey gasped as she shifted toward him. "Of course I believed him. Why wouldn't I?"

"There is the issue of him running off to a foreign country with another woman. And not just any woman—an actress."

"Carlina Leoni can't act her way out of a paper bag." Joey slapped a hand across her mouth.

"Finally we agree on something."

"Didn't you just do…seems I remember reading—"

"Yes, Ms. Leoni and I have a working relationship. I still full-heartedly agree with your assessment."

She smiled. "Like I was saying. After I listened to Laurence's voice mail—"

"You mean Larry?"

"Laurence. He doesn't like being called Larry."

"Sort of how you don't like being called Jo-Jo?"

"I don't mind…too much." She shrugged through the obvious lie. "We're getting off the subject." Joey cleared her throat. "After I listened to Laurence's voice mail and he said that he loved me, I knew his breaking up with me, the sudden engagement and the impulsive vacation to Italy all equal one thing," she concluded smiling.

"Midlife crisis," he guessed.

Joey's eyes widened. "You think so, too?" Hope shimmered in her eyes.

"So, let me get this straight." Ryan chuckled, edging closer to her. "You're just going to show up in Italy like this—" he quickly gestured to her plain attire "—with your arms open wide and say 'I love you, Larry. Please choose me over Hollywood's hottest actress.'"

She swallowed. "Hottest actress?"

"*Candyland* opened number one at the box office this weekend." He lowered his voice to add. "Trust me. It wasn't because it was a good film."

Joey shifted in her chair, while doubt carved lines across her forehead. Then just as suddenly her confidence charged back into her features while her shoulders lifted. "He'll choose me. I'm loyal, dependable and have more class than Carlina Leoni, who can't seem to keep her business from being broadcast across the Internet."

"Well, good luck to you." He finally returned to his script. "You're going to need it."

"Luck will have nothing to do with it." He saw her chin rise to a ridiculous level.

Ryan stared at her without being obvious. He hadn't lied when he said that he liked this toned-down version of her. She looked softer, adorable and obtainable. He thought about Larry and wondered how he could choose a narcissist like Carlina Leoni over Joey. *Has to be going through a midlife crisis.*

"Are you a workaholic?" Joey asked, glancing at the paperwork still strewed across his lap.

His lips sloped unevenly as he slid on his glasses. "Something like that."

"You probably get tired of people coming up to you and pitching their ideas to you, huh?"

He glanced over and saw the hope shining in her eyes. "There's a lot of legal reasons behind it," he said, letting her down easy. "If I end up making a script similar to yours, lawsuits fly…"

"Yeah, yeah." She nodded through her disappointment. "I figured as much."

"But you can have your agent send me something and I'll make sure I take a peek at it."

"Yeah, sure."

Ryan shrugged and pretended that her sudden indifference didn't bother him. He shuffled his paperwork again, kept pretending he wasn't watching her and longed for another conversation starter. However, Joey seemed just as determined to ignore him.

Minutes after returning home from her morning spa trip, Frankie zonked out on the sofa before Rosa, her maid, brought her a cup of her favorite chamomile tea. This was starting to become a habit after spending an hour with Miguel and his wonderful massaging hands. Just thinking about them had her moaning in her sleep.

The phone rang, wrenching Frankie out of her fantasy and spoiling her mood. "Hello."

"Hello. May I speak with a Franklin Lee Adams?"

Frankie sat up. It had been years since anyone had called her by her maiden name. "This is Ms. Adams. What can I do for you?"

"I'm Mrs. Crane. I'm calling from American Express. We're showing unusual activity on your credit card."

"My credit card?"

"Yes, ma'am. We're showing a transaction for $2,644 for—"

"What?"

"Were you not aware of this purchase?"

"I most certainly was not!"

"Would you like for us to post a fraud alert and freeze all activity on this card?"

"Damn right I do!"

* * *

Joey's eyes snapped open when her plane hit "a little turbulence." How long had she been asleep? If they were going to crash, maybe it was best that she went back to sleep. What about her family? No one knew where she was.

"Excuse me?" Ryan cleared his throat.

She glanced over and groaned.

"Do you think you could let go of my hand? Your nails have hit bone."

She lowered her gaze. "No, I don't think so," she said unable to loosen her grip.

The plane hit another air pocket, and Joey finally released him long enough for her arms to wrench around his neck and for her to actually meld her body against his.

"'Somewhere, over the rainbow…'"

"Ms. Adams, what are you doing?" He pretended that his body wasn't going haywire from her touch.

"Way up high…"

"We're *not* crashing, Joey!" he hissed under his breath, and then waited.

"We're not?"

"No." He sighed in relief when he felt her arms relax and air was finally allowed to flow back into his body.

"Are you sure?"

Ryan reached up and pried her arms off him. "You know you don't have to try so hard to get my attention. You have a standing invitation to my hotel room."

Joey leaped away from him. "You're disgusting."

"What happened to just being an asshole?"

"You've surpassed that threshold." She huffed and

folded her arms. "You've made it quite clear that you're only interested in sleeping with me. I get it. You can stop hinting. My answer is still 'no.'"

"A lot of women would be flattered."

"I'm not a lot of women." She straightened and composed herself. "I have a little more dignity and self-respect."

He frowned. "Did you forget how we met?"

"Fine. Fine. I did one stupid thing."

"Are we not counting this surprise trip to Italy on your ex-boyfriend who is currently engaged to a hot actress?"

"No, we're not," she hissed.

"You mean 'not yet.'"

Joey's eyes lowered to thin slits. "Can you do me a favor and not talk to me for the rest of this trip?"

"Only if you promise not to leap back into my lap. Next time you might get a little surprise." He winked.

"I take it *little* is the key word there."

"Oh, the kitten has claws." He laughed, enjoying their repartee. He didn't know why but he enjoyed getting under her skin.

"Do we have a deal?" she asked.

"Deal."

For the rest of flight, Joey and Ryan zipped up their lips and pretended to ignore each other.

Inwardly, however, Joey ranted about the famed director's incredible ego. The casting couch was probably the only way he could get a date. And she had kissed him.

Landing was the hardest part for Joey. She clutched her chair, slammed her eyes shut and hummed her rainbow song. When they were safely on the ground, she relaxed and said a quick prayer of thanks.

"I guess this is goodbye," Ryan said, standing.

Her eyes flashed at him.

"What? I kept my promise. The trip is over."

Joey kept her mouth clammed tight.

"Well, for what it's worth," he went on to say as he grabbed his overhead bag, "I wish you the best of luck with Dr. Benson."

She remained suspicious.

"I'm actually starting to believe you two are meant for each other."

"Thank you." She lifted her chin. "And good luck to you and your new movie. Judging by your recent track record, you're going to need it."

Ryan laughed and exited the plane.

Joey also grabbed her bag and made her way off the aircraft. She rushed through the maze of Linate Airport and hailed a taxi.

"Hotel Principe di Savoia Milano, *per favore*."

"Si, signora."

Joey smiled and turned her head back toward the airport. Was she expecting to see Ryan Donovan again? She shook her head as her cab pulled off. With any luck she had seen the last of Mr. Donovan.

Chapter 12

"I don't understand. Ronald is a cool guy. Why won't your brother go out with him?" Lincoln asked, cramming the fifth suitcase into the trunk of his car.

Peyton smiled. "You really do care for my brother's happiness, don't you?"

"Of course I care. Why wouldn't I?" He slammed the trunk shut and then draped an arm around his wife. "He's family."

She glided her arms around his trim waist and then leaned up on her toes for a kiss. "Don't take it personally, honey. I'm sure Ronald is a wonderful guy and all, but don't forget Flex lives in Atlanta. The last thing he would want is to get involved in a long-distance relationship." She gave him another kiss.

Lincoln thought it over and shrugged at the logic. "I

guess that means I'll have to let Ronald down easy." He cringed. "That's gonna be awkward."

"It's not easy playing Cupid."

"Speaking from experience?"

"More like a witness to every bad idea and plan my sisters had ever come up with. And trust me, there have been a lot of them."

"Hey," Marlin yelled from the front porch. "You two heading out?"

Lincoln and Peyton linked their arms together and walked back toward the house.

"I'm afraid so," Lincoln said. "House renovations should be completed today. I want to thank you again for your hospitality."

"No need to thank me. This will always be you guys' second home." Marlin winked.

A car pulled up into the driveway and everyone turned to see Michael's Volvo.

Peyton waved and then broke away from Lincoln. She'd been more than a little concerned about Michael ever since Phillip's call Saturday morning. Peyton had also expected Michael to rush home once word of Flex's visit hit the Sisters' Network. Even their father had noted the oddity.

Michael climbed out of the car, flashed a high-wattage smile and waved. "Hey, everybody."

"Where have you been?" Peyton asked, taking her sister into her arms for a quick embrace. "I was beginning to think I was going to have to round up a search party." She glanced into the car. "Where's Joey?"

"She's not here?"

Peyton frowned. "No. I thought she disappeared with you."

Worry instantly creased Michael's brow. "Dear God, I hope she hasn't done something stupid."

Twenty-four hours in Milan, Italy, and Dr. Laurence Benson was miserable. The beautiful high-fashion city felt like an icicle in February, and each time he saw his swollen jaw in the mirror, he thought of Joey.

Beautiful, tomboyish Joey had expected an engagement ring for Valentine's Day—and he had almost given it to her. Joey had his heart, but Carlina was the logical choice.

The train of his thoughts was derailed when Carlina emerged from their suite's bathroom. She was dressed stunningly from head to toe in winter white. It might be a cliché, but she looked the part of the perfect trophy wife. Plus, it wouldn't hurt his practice to be married to Hollywood's "it" girl.

"How do I look?" Carlina asked, spinning around for inspection.

"The way you always look…magnificent!" He went to her with open arms. "Let me guess. You're all set to go shopping?"

"Well, there are only ten days before the wedding and I have a ton of things to do." She tweaked his cheek and walked over to the bed to pick up her purse. "Are you sure you don't mind my going out with old school friends?"

"No. Have some fun. I'll be fine," he said.

"Great. I'll try not to stay out too late. We're having breakfast with my parents in the morning."

"I'll be ready." He winked and held on to his smile

until she walked out of the door. "What am I doing?" he moaned. He quickly made himself a drink at the bar and then strolled over to the window. "Joey, Joey, Joey." He squinted down at a woman in the courtyard. "Joey?" He thought about it for a moment and shook his head. "Nah. It couldn't be."

The moment Joey walked into Hotel Principe di Savoia Milano, she felt as if she'd been transported to another time and place where kings and queens ruled the world and she was in the company of royalty. She eased down the marbled entryway, feeling as if she stuck out like a sore thumb.

In truth, she did.

At the front desk, a tall, lanky Italian man with the shiniest black hair she'd ever seen turned toward her. *"Posso aiutarla, signora?"*

"I'm sorry, but I speak very little Italian," Joey informed him.

"Of course." His smile brightened. "May I help you, madame?"

"Yes, I have a reservation for Joseph Adams."

The clerk's skinny fingers glided across his computer keyboard. "Yes, I show we have one suite reserved for a Signore Adams."

"Actually, it's Signora Adams. I'm Joseph."

The young man's eyebrows dipped together in confusion. "Joseph is a man, no?"

"No. In this case, Joseph is a girl." She pulled out her passport and showed it to him. He studied the passport, but his expression remained the same until she admitted, "My father was hoping for a boy."

"Ah." He flashed her a tight smile, and then resumed typing. "I show one junior suite, single use is eight hundred and twenty-five American dollars and—"

"A night?"

"*Si, signora.* Will that be a problem?"

A frog leaped into Joey's throat in time for her to croak, "No."

"Excellent." A smile returned to his face before he asked how she would like to pay for the room.

Joey nervously fished through her purse and pulled out her wallet. She held her breath as she withdrew Frankie's credit card and handed it over to the clerk.

"Just one moment," he said, and slid the card down a magnetic strip next to his computer.

She tapped her fingers across the countertop until the clerk flashed her a look of annoyance. "Sorry."

He punched a few buttons and slid the card down again.

Joey's heart threatened to burst through her chest cavity. The other two credit cards she possessed were just hairs away from their maximum and would certainly decline. One thing was for sure, she didn't have a whole lot of time to win Laurence back.

"*Spiacente,* Signora Adams, but your credit card has been declined," the tall, lanky desk clerk informed her. "We have been instructed to destroy the card."

"What?" Panic seized Joey. "You can't do that. That is the only credit card I have. I don't have any money."

He produced a pair of scissors and sliced the card in half before she could even think to stop him. "Does that mean that you'll be canceling your reservation?"

She blinked. "Er, huh."

"Signora?"

"How long can you hold the room?"

"*Spiacente.* We'll need a credit card in order to hold the suite. And unfortunately it is now the only suite we have available. So if anyone asks for it *and* can actually *pay* for the suite, we will give it to them."

A woman snickered behind Joey, and she could literally feel herself shrink a few inches. "Thank you," she muttered and turned away from the front desk.

Now what?

She walked back down the marbled entryway toward the front door with her head down. She had to think of something. She hadn't come all this way to be turned down. Hell, without Frankie's credit card, she couldn't even afford a plane ticket back home.

Calling home wasn't an option. Her sisters would haul her back so fast her head would spin. She couldn't allow that—not until she spoke with Laurence.

Stepping out of the building, Joey glanced up at the towering palatial hotel. She was an ant who'd barely escaped being squashed. "I am no quitter," she mumbled under her breath and then marched back into the hotel.

When she reached the front desk, the clerk turned and greeted her with another magnanimous smile. "Ah, Ms. Adams. You returned—with money, I hope?"

She mimicked his smile. "No. Actually, I was hoping you could give me Dr. Laurence Benson's suite number? He's my fiancé."

One of the clerk's bushy eyebrows rose to the center of his forehead. "Dr. Benson is *your* fiancé?"

"Yes," she lied with a straight face.

The clerk's face remained dubious and his voice obnoxiously polite. "*Spiacente, signora.* If Dr. Benson is indeed a guest at our hotel, his privacy is of utmost importance with the staff of Principe di Savoia Milano."

"You won't tell me his room number?"

"As you Americans say, 'Bingo.'"

When he smiled, Joey wondered what the consequences would be if she knocked his block off.

"Anything else?" he asked.

"No. I guess not." She leveled him with her best evil glare.

"Very well."

He turned and left her to glower at his back. She left the front desk in yet another huff. *Think, think.* The only cash she had was used on the cab ride, and the driver was none too thrilled to take American dollars. Planning ahead had never been her strong suit.

Once again she stood outside the grand hotel without a man, a plan or a clue what do next.

"One thing for sure," she mumbled under her breath. "This trip can't get any worse."

Chapter 13

Things got worse. A whole lot worse.

Hours after getting the boot from the hotel, Joey decided to find a small café so she could gather her thoughts and devise a new plan. Certainly she had enough money on one of her other credit cards for a cup of coffee.

"Thief! Thief!" the café owner shouted.

"No, no." Joey frantically looked all around her small table. "Someone stole my purse. I placed it right here." She gestured to the floor underneath her table. "Someone must have stolen it."

"Chiamare la polizia!"

Joey's limited Italian certainly recognized the word police. Another jaunt in jail, this time in a foreign one, held little appeal. "Please, please. I swear someone has stolen my purse."

All eyes in the small café zeroed in on the loud commotion. Joey's ears heated with embarrassment, but her humiliation grew in leaps and bounds when the police arrived.

The café owner and the *polizia* acted like they didn't buy her story, especially since neither she nor the other patrons had witnessed the theft.

She dug into her jeans and her one suitcase until she found a five-dollar bill in her packed denim jacket. The burly café owner snatched the money and had the *polizia* escort her off the property.

It didn't occur to her until after the incident and the cops were gone that she still had a major problem.

No credit cards, no money, no passport and no cell phone.

That was two days ago.

Last night while she was sound asleep on a public bench, another crook managed to steal her one suitcase.

At this moment Joey was convinced that she would sell her soul for a Tic Tac. The country may be beautiful, but the locals didn't look too kindly upon the homeless, and it was getting harder and harder to mask that was what she was: homeless, or rather hotelless.

Since cell phones ruled the world, Joey was amazed how difficult it was to find a single payphone in the whole damn town. By the time she found one, she didn't know what she should tell her family. If she called and told them what she did, her sisters would be on the next thing smokin' to Italy. Call her crazy, but she wasn't ready for that. Not yet.

And then she saw him: Dr. Laurence Benson, her ex-almost-fiancé. She spotted him and Ms. Boob Job exiting Principe di Savoia Milano. They were arm in arm, smiling and laughing about something—probably Joey. Chances were that all of Milan was talking about the foreign black American girl who stole coffee and slept on public benches.

She sighed as she stared at them. They were the pinup interracial power couple and looked like they'd recently enjoyed a hot shower.

Joey's face twisted with misery. She wanted a hot shower, too. She was beginning to offend herself. More important, she couldn't approach Laurence looking the way she looked or smelling the way she smelled.

She needed another plan—one that would actually work.

As night descended…again, she struggled to remember how long a body could go without food. Not to mention how cold it was at night. Instead of falling asleep, Joey felt more as though she was being induced into a coma.

If she committed a crime, at least she would be able to sleep indoors for a night. She walked with no destination in mind, but her stomach followed the wonderful aromas wafting from a nearby restaurant.

She approached and plastered her face against the restaurant's glass walls. The elegantly dressed men and women dined merrily off plates that looked more like works of art than dinner. Joey drew a deep breath and imagined what the food must taste like and how smooth the wine would flow down her parched throat.

She closed her eyes and let her imagination go wild.

"Will you just look at that woman?"

Ryan turned his head, and his gaze followed where

most of the patrons stared at a woman writhing against the window.

"What the hell do you think she's doing?" Zach asked.

"I don't know." Ryan squinted. "But I think I know her." He pushed back in his chair and tossed the napkin from his lap onto the table. "Excuse me for a minute, won't you?"

"Ryan—"

"I'll be back," he said absently, and stood. As he made a beeline from his table to the front door, he tried to convince himself that the woman outside the restaurant was not, could not be who he thought it was.

Stepping out into the cold night, Ryan's footsteps slowed as his heart sank. "Joey?"

Her head jerked back and her eyes zoomed toward him.

Ryan blinked. "Oh, my God. It is you." He rushed over to her. "What happened?"

"Ryan?" She said his name as though she was almost afraid to believe. "Is that you?"

He reached out and touched her matted hair, while his gaze took in her dirt-smudged face and the large bags under her eyes. "You look…"

She hand-pressed her hair down and buttoned her denim jacket.

"…different," he settled on saying.

"Well, I know I'm not exactly presentable at the moment." She laughed weakly and then frowned. "What are you doing here?"

"Eating."

"Oh." Her eyes turned dreamy. "That sounds nice."

He cocked his head, while he warred with whether

to be amused or concerned. "Would—would you like
to join me for dinner?"

Joey's hand shook as it fluttered to her throat. "I…I
don't think I should. I, uh…" She glanced back toward
the window and was astonished to see she had an
audience. "Thank you—no."

Her stomach growled in protest—and it wasn't a
little growl. It was a long mountain lion that went on
for a full thirty seconds.

"You know—" Ryan reached into his dinner jacket
and removed a cigar "—you can't eat your pride."

She stared at him, warring with whether she looked
at an angel or the devil. "I don't have any money," she
confessed while her ears burned in protest.

"I think I can cover the tab."

She held up her chin, thinking of all his past sexual
innuendos. "What's it going to cost me?"

"I probably deserved that." He also lifted his chin
and lit his cigar. "Tell you what. Dinner is on me. No
strings attached. You have my word as a gentleman."

Her eyes narrowed.

"I can even put it in writing if you like."

Joey smiled, but before she could respond to his
offer the mountain lion returned.

"C'mon," he said, taking her by the arm. "I'll never
forgive myself if I let you stand out here and starve to
death."

She allowed him to tug her into the restaurant. Once
inside, the diners issued a round of applause and completed Joey's embarrassment.

"I think introductions are in order." Ryan held out a
chair. "Zachary Griffin, Joey Adams. Joey, Zach."

"Nice to meet you." Joey smiled without showing her teeth. After all, it had been three days since she had brushed them.

"The pleasure is all mine." Zach's gaze held a trunk-load of questions while it shifted to Ryan.

Ryan smiled and signaled for the waiter. "Bring us a bottle of your best white Pinot."

"Very good, sir." The waiter scampered off.

Joey's eyes landed on the untouched baked bread in the center of the table. Her fingers inched to snatch it and shove the entire thing down her throat.

"Help yourself," Ryan gestured.

She told herself to gently reach for the bread, but what happened was more like an attack. She tore, shoved, crammed and nearly choked on the soft bread.

Horrified, Zach stared.

Fascinated, Ryan hid his smile behind the back of his hand.

The waiter returned cautiously with their wine. His expression a barely controlled masked of concern.

"Thank you," Ryan said, and signaled for him to pour Joey a glass.

The minute he filled it, Joey snatched her glass and chugged it down like a seasoned college frat student.

"So, how is it that you two know each other?" Zach asked, unable to pulled his gaze away from their guest.

"We met in a men's room," Ryan said.

Zach finally jerked his gaze to Ryan. "Come again?"

Joey came up for air. "It's not as seedy as he's making it sound. I was trying to break into the Blue Diamond in Los Angeles."

"Oh, well. That's much better." He frowned and continued to stare at his friend. "Not seedy at all."

However, Ryan seemed content to stare at Joey.

The waiter cleared his throat. "Are you ready to order?"

"Give us a few more minutes. Ms. Adams hasn't had a chance to decide." He handed her the menu.

Joey hesitated while her eyes glossed with tears. *Food.*

"Trust me." Ryan winked. "We ate here last night. The food is divine."

Accepting the menu, she leaned forward and whispered, "I promise. I will pay you back."

Damn right you will. Ryan smiled.

Joey's greedy eyes roamed over the eight-page menu. Each dish sounded better than the last. For a moment she had a renegade thought of ordering everything.

The waiter returned to the table four times only to be told that they needed a few more minutes.

"How about I choose something for you?" Ryan asked after feeling his own hunger rise.

"Maybe that is best," she agreed, and handed back the menu.

Zach placed everyone's order while Joey attacked the second loaf of bread delivered to the table.

"It's nice seeing a woman who's not afraid of carbohydrates for a change," Zach said, lightening the mood.

Ryan chuckled. "I happen to like a woman with a healthy appetite."

Zach's eyebrows leaped to the center of his forehead.

"You like anything with breasts and a pulse," Joey mumbled.

"Ow." Ryan dramatically withdrew an imaginary knife from his chest. "An unprovoked attack."

Suddenly ashamed and embarrassed by her thoughtless barb, Joey reached for his hand. The moment she touched him another crackle of kinetic energy surged through her and she quickly snatched her hand back.

"I'm sorry." She cleared her throat. "I shouldn't have said that."

"Forget about it." He eyed her as he puffed on his cigar. "Sooo. How are things with you and the great Dr. Benson?"

Joey shrank a little in her chair as she glanced at Zach. "I don't want to talk about it."

"Now I officially feel like the third wheel."

A team of waiters appeared with their meals.

"I think I would just like to have mine in a doggy bag," Zach informed their main waiter.

"As you wish, sir."

"No." Joey sat up straight. "Please, you don't have to leave on my account."

"It's okay. I have an early day tomorrow and it seems you two have a lot to catch up on."

"But—"

"I'll see you in the morning." Ryan smiled, unable to hide his pleasure at being left alone with Joey from his friend's well-trained eye.

"Yes, we have a lot to…go over in the morning." Zach stood. "It was nice meeting you, Ms. Adams. Maybe I'll see you around again?"

"Not likely, but then again I can't seem to shake Mr. Donovan, either."

"And here I thought I was growing on you," Ryan snickered.

"Actually, I'm starting to think that you're some kind of guardian angel," she confessed, reaching for her glass of wine.

"I may be a lot of things, Joey. But I'm no angel."

"Amen." Zach laughed and walked off before Ryan could toss back a rebuttal.

"Would the *signora* like to add some cheese?" the waiter asked.

"Yes, please." Joey's eyes widened at the serving size of her pasta dish. She let the waiter grate a ridiculous amount of cheese on her meal before calling a halt.

Ryan lost interest in his own food. He became amazed on just how much a small woman could eat. "You don't have a tape worm or something do you?"

"Uh?" Joey dabbed her mouth but kept going. "What did you say?"

"Nothing." He propped an elbow up on the table and just watched. Twenty minutes later her plate was empty and he had a sneaking suspicion that if he weren't sitting there, she would lick the plate.

Finally he leaned forward and braided his fingers beneath his chin. "I take it the food met your approval?"

"It was the best meal I've ever had." Dropping back against her chair, she unabashedly undid the top button of her jeans.

"No room for dessert?" he asked, taking the first bite of his meal.

She moaned as her eyes turned dreamy again. "I think I can squeeze in some cheesecake."

"Then let's get you some." He started to lift his hand, but then thought better of it. "On one condition."

"I knew it." Her eyes narrowed. "What happened to that stuff about being a gentleman? Well, you can forget it. I'm not sleeping with you for some lousy slice of cheesecake." Though I might consider it for a hot bath.

"On the condition that you tell me what happened to you and Dr. Benson."

She certainly didn't see a problem in that. "You have yourself a deal.

Chapter 14

The Adams family was seized with worry. Each individual called every acquaintance, friend and boyfriend Joey had ever had—twice. All with no luck.

LAPD requested a recent picture and was given enough photos to papier-mâché the whole precinct. Still nothing.

"She has to be at a conference or something," Peyton reasoned aloud as she stepped away from Joey's wardrobe closet.

"Then why isn't she returning our calls?" Michael challenged in a voice tight with fright. "We've left at least a hundred calls on her cell phone."

"Maybe she's somewhere she doesn't want us to know about?" Flex interjected. Worry set deep grooved lines into his forehead and around his eyes. "Joey can be very secretive at times."

"You mean she can be a little flighty."

"Sheldon!" Frankie snapped.

"What?" Sheldon rubbed her belly. "Joseph has a problem of not thinking things through before she does them. That's no big secret. We all know that."

No one spoke, in silent affirmation.

Lincoln knocked on Joey's open bedroom door before he entered and handed a steaming cup of coffee over to his wife. "I just brewed a fresh pot if anyone is interested."

Everyone nodded their heads and filed out of the junky room.

"How are you holding up?" Lincoln asked Peyton.

"Still warring with myself about whether we're over-reacting." She sipped her coffee and relished the instant warmth added to her body. "Joey could've just forgotten to tell us about a business trip."

Smiling, Lincoln slid his muscled arm around her waist. "It's more than likely."

She nodded and gently pulled out of his arms to follow her sisters to the living room.

In their overzealous concern, the family had ransacked the place for clues as to Joey's whereabouts. Now Peyton grew concerned about Joey hitting the roof when she saw the place.

"Maybe we should clean up?" Peyton suggested, glancing around.

Everyone followed her gaze and looked as though it was the first time they noticed the mess.

"Couldn't we just *hire* someone?" Frankie asked.

The rest of the family rolled their eyes and went to

work. Frankie's allergies to manual labor were well known.

Marlin sat mute on the sofa. As the patriarch he remained calm and reserved. In the past three days he'd also held the opinion that Joey was just being Joey.

After all, last year Joey had moved to Los Angles from San Jose without saying a word to anyone. It was Joey's way of avoiding the sisters' network where everyone expressed their opinions of what someone should or should not do with their own lives.

Even Flex had been a victim of the maneuver— that's why he moved to Georgia.

Nevertheless, Sheldon, Frankie, Michael and Peyton always sounded the alarm when a member of the family broke protocol or abandoned ship.

Marlin just hoped to make it back home in time for his poker night.

Flex grabbed a few cushions from the floor and tables and returned them to the appropriate chairs. He picked up a throw pillow from an end table and noticed the answering machine's flashing red light.

"Did anyone check Joey's machine?"

"Hell, I know I left several messages," Peyton said, returning books to the bookshelf.

"We all have," Sheldon amended, removing the vacuum cleaner from the hall closet.

He shrugged. "Yeah, but there may be a clue on here where Joey has gone." Flex pushed the play button.

You have fifty new messages. This mailbox is full. Please delete your messages.

Michael laughed. "I guess we left more than a few messages."

"Hello, Jo-Jo. It's Laurence…"

"Oh, hell," Frankie murmured. "Did anyone call this jerk?"

"He's out of town," Michael replied, her own dread seeping into her voice.

Everyone fell silent as they inched closer to the answer machine.

"Joey, are you there? Pick up." Laurence's deep exhalation floated over the recorder. "I, uh, oh hell. I don't really know where to begin—other than tonight when I saw you, I don't know."

Michael rolled her eyes. "I think I'm going to be sick."

"Shhh!" the family hissed.

"I'm confused," Laurence admitted. "I thought I'd made the right decision…but now—I'm not so sure. I mean, this is crazy, I leave for Milan tomorrow and—" he sighed "—I think…I still having feelings for you…I mean I still *love* you and—"

"Laarrry."

"Larry?" Sheldon glanced at everyone. "Who in the hell is calling him Larry?"

"Shhh!"

"I'm coming," Laurence's muffled voice called back, but then it turned crystal clear when he spoke back into the mouthpiece. "Look, Joey. I better go." There was a long pause before he added. "Bye."

Peyton hit the stop button. "Did he say something about Milan?"

"As in Italy?" Sheldon asked.

"She couldn't have gone to Italy. She doesn't have that kind of money," Michael reasoned.

Frankie eyes bulged.

"Yeah, you're right," Peyton nodded. "She wouldn't have."

"She couldn't have," Sheldon agreed.

Frankie dropped her head into the palms of her hands and croaked, "She did."

"So let me get this straight." Ryan adjusted his weight in his chair. "You've been here for three days and you haven't talk to him yet?"

Joey bit into her second slice of cheesecake and moaned as if her soul had a G-spot.

Ryan made another adjustment in his chair. Despite looking as if she'd slept the last three days in a gutter, she still was able to get the blood pumping in all areas of his body.

And that was a good thing.

"I haven't spoken to him yet—but I will."

"Let me guess. You have a plan." Ryan chuckled while his eyes danced around her beautiful face.

"Actually, I'm still working on one."

He wrinkled his nose. "Does it include a shower?"

Her next bite of dessert stopped inches from her mouth. "What are you saying?"

"I'm saying, *sweetheart,* that you stink." He plopped his cigar back into his mouth, and then added, "Badly."

Joey swallowed a hard lump of air and dropped her fork. When silver hit glass, it caused a loud clatter and drew a few more eyeballs in Ryan and Joey's direction. "I better go." She pushed back her chair and cringed when it screeched across the floor.

More eyes followed.

She jumped up from her seat with her entire body ablaze with embarrassment.

"Wait." Ryan snuffed out his cigar, and chucked his white linen napkin onto the table. "You don't have to go." His words hit her racing back. "Damn it."

Scooping out his money clip, he tossed more than enough money to cover his tab and bolted after Joey.

Icy winds sliced through his clothes and he fleetingly thought to return to the restaurant for his coat and gloves, but then caught sight of Joey racing down the street.

"Where in the hell is she going?" he mumbled, taking off after her. His long athletic legs erased the distance between them in no time. When he caught up, he only smiled at her long string of curses.

"Damn, damn, damn. It's cold," she huffed, and then clutched at her sides.

"You know, it's not a good idea to run on a full stomach. At least that's what my mother used to tell me." Ryan slowed his stride to keep pace with her.

She rolled her eyes, but then stopped in her tracks and doubled over.

Shaking his head, Ryan backtracked and stopped next to her. "Cramp?"

Out of pride, she shook her head. In the next second her muscles clenched tighter and she was forced to nod the truth.

Another chuckle tumbled from Ryan's lips.

"I'm so glad I amuse you," she hissed.

He thought about placating her. "Well, you have to admit you're a little bit high-strung."

"What?" She attempted to straighten up; however, her sore muscles had other plans and she remained doubled over. "One plane flight of conversation doesn't mean you know everything about me." Her teeth chattered as a strong gust of wind nearly caused her to kiss the ground.

"Correction—one bathroom rescue, one *long* plane flight and one dinner date."

Finally her side muscles relaxed and she rose out of her right-angle position. "Tonight was not a date."

"Did you pay for dinner?"

"I *told* you I didn't have any money!"

"Then it was a date."

"You said no strings attached," she accused.

"I haven't attached any." He shrugged, still unable to remove the smile from his lips. "It was a nice meal with good conversation—the end."

She looked as though she was chewing nails before she spat out, "You insulted me."

"I, as a friend, told you the truth. Your BO lit up the joint."

"I…well…see…" Joey's face crumpled. "Oh my God." Tears leaked from her eyes. "I *do* stink." She buried her face in the palms of her hands and wept.

Feeling awkward and inadequate, Ryan brought her trembling shoulders into his embrace—in part for some body heat and in part because he liked touching her.

"Sooo," he said, stroking her back and feeling his erection harden against his thigh. "Why don't you come back to my hotel suite?"

She stopped crying and pulled back.

Ryan surrendered his hands into the air. "Just so you can take a shower."

Her eyes narrowed, but her body hummed at the idea of being able to stand beneath a jet of streaming hot water. "Just for a shower?" she asked for clarification.

"Just for a shower," he agreed, smiling.

If it looks like a snake and hisses like a snake, chances were she was dealing with a snake—and a shower.

"What hotel are you staying in?"

"Hotel Principe di Savoia Milano."

A warm, genuine smile eased across Joey's dirt-smudged face. "Mr. Donovan, I would love to go your hotel suite."

Chapter 15

Ryan was minutes away from getting laid. He was certain of it the moment he ushered Joey into the elegant, fifty-four-hundred-square-foot presidential suite, and he slid on his Casanova act.

"Wow. This place is *really* nice," Joey gushed as her gaze danced from the grand piano to the lacunar ceiling and the large terrace with a panoramic view of Milan. "You even have a fireplace."

"Perfect for wintry nights." He inched closer.

She rolled her eyes at his lame theatrics, instantly signaling him to step up his game.

"Would you like a private tour?"

Joey shook her head. "Maybe after the shower."

"Suit yourself." He shrugged and led her across the marble floor to the enormously grand bathroom. "I'm sure you'll find everything you need in here. There are a few robes on the rack. "Help yourself."

She smiled and stepped into the bathroom and stopped. "Thank you." Joey turned and faced him. "For everything."

Ryan blinked. For a moment he felt guilty about his hidden agenda for a vulnerable woman. What kind of man would prey on a woman stuck in a foreign country with no money, no clothes and no place to stay?

He would—especially to end his current little... problem.

"It's no big deal," he said slyly.

She flashed him another smile and closed the door.

He laid his head against the partition and expelled a long breath. At the sound of the shower, he turned with a wide smile.

Just a few more minutes, he promised himself.

He pulled off his coat and unfastened the top three buttons of his shirt while he made a beeline toward the fireplace. In no time at all, a fire crackled to life and room service arrived on cue.

"Here's a little something extra for you." Ryan slipped the man his tip.

The young man's eyes lit up. *"Grazie, signore. Grazie."*

Ryan smiled and guided the server out the door. He retrieved a blanket from one of the bedrooms and laid it before the fire. From his laptop, he retrieved the only CD he had, *Luther Vandross's Greatest Hits,* and popped it into the stereo system.

Now the stage was set for seduction.

Joey stood on weak knees beneath the best showerhead in the world. Water pounded and massaged her skin to the point she didn't care to ever leave. She lathered and rinsed, lathered and rinsed until the small square hotel soap disappeared and her fingertips pickled.

Reluctantly she shut off the shower. When she stepped out and reached for a towel, her ears perked at Luther's unmistakable voice.

She frowned. There's only one reason a man puts Luther Vandross on the stereo. "No strings attached, my ass."

Joey snatched one of the hotel robes from the rack. The large fluffy material swallowed her small frame, and the belt circled her waist twice. Steam billowed out the bathroom as she eased out the door.

"Well, if it isn't the cleanest woman in all of Italy," Ryan said from behind the piano bench. He lifted a champagne glass. "Drink?"

Joey had never seen a more obvious wolf in sheep's clothing. Her gaze skittered from him to the lit fireplace, the low lighting, and his identical terry-cloth robe. "It's not going to happen," she warned.

"What?"

His eyes grew a little too wide to pull off the innocent look, but she was charmed just the same. "I'm not sleeping with you."

His Cheshire Cat smile grew wider as he popped his cigar in his mouth. "If you say so."

"Has anyone ever told you that's a nasty habit you have there?"

"What?" He removed the cigar and glanced at it. "This?"

Joey folded her arms as she crossed the room. "Smoking causes lung cancer."

"What are you, my mother?" He winked. "Do you want to spank me?" He placed the cigar in a glass ashtray.

She shook her head, still charmed. "Does this act really work on women?"

"You tell me." Ryan stood and approached with a flute of champagne extended out to her. His walk was too confident, his smile too wide—but he couldn't seem to tone down his performance. He was anxious to score a home run despite his inability to step into the batter's box with this woman.

Joey accepted the glass with a smile and then turned toward the fireplace. "Sooo. How's preproduction going?" she asked idly.

He kept his silly smile in place while he followed her. "It's coming along."

"A blanket, huh?"

Ryan shrugged. "No harm in getting comfortable."

She shook her head. "Your nose is growing, Pinocchio."

"You're not exactly Honest Abe, Ms. Adams." He clinked their flutes of champagne together while his heavy gaze caressed her face. "You keep saying no but…"

Her eyebrows seesawed with curiosity. "But what?"

"But you are standing in the middle of my hotel suite, freshly showered, in my robe and sipping champagne before a roaring fire. There is a word men call women like you."

She lifted her head and clenched her jaw. "And what is that?"

"A tease."

"That's two words."

"So it is." Ryan chuckled. "But you *are* a tease."

Joey opened her mouth to argue; but at the last moment, she flashed him a stunning smile and sipped her drink.

"Does that mean I have permission to stamp guilty on your forehead?"

"I plead the fifth." She winked, enjoying how easily she wrapped him around her finger. How come Laurence never fawned over her this way?

Because he has an affinity for silicon breasts instead of the real McCoy.

"Why don't we sit down?"

She hesitated.

"I won't bite."

Joey lowered herself onto the blanket, but slowly her smile ebbed away as she thought about the past week—really thought about it. "What am I doing?" She sighed. "What am I doing here?"

"We're getting acquainted." He clinked their glasses again and resumed pouring on the charm.

"No. I mean what am I doing here in Italy, chasing after a man who dumped me?" She set her glass down on the fireplace mantel and cupped her face in her hands. "When did I become so desperate?"

"Now, now." Ryan strategically placed an arm around her shoulder to showcase the appropriate amount of sympathy. "Don't be hard on yourself. Your ex-fiancé sort of led you on."

"Ex-almost-fiancé," she corrected.

"Right, right. That's what I meant." He set his glass

down next to hers in order to massage her shoulders. "But you know it's never too late to put the whole thing behind you—to move on."

Joey closed her eyes and emitted a soft moan. "You have nice hands."

He leaned close to whisper in her ear. "I'm glad you like them." He allowed a moment of silence to pass before he added, "I have other nice things, you know."

She chuckled and emerged from her pool of self-pity. "I'm not interested in your other 'nice things.'" She turned around to face him, but was momentarily taken aback when her eyes met his beautiful unblinking stare.

"You feel it, too. Don't you?" he asked, gently sliding the backs of his fingers down her supple cheek.

She should respond—say something else sarcastic—but the truth was, she did feel...something.

"I love Larry." Joey blinked. "I mean *Laurence*." She straightened her spine and pulled away from his touch.

Ryan's tone remained soft but firm. "Laurence is with Carlina. His current fiancée."

Instantly tears sprang to her eyes and he quickly, gently wiped them away. "Maybe fate is what brought you here—brought *us* here."

"You're better at this than I thought," she whispered.

"I've never been this inspired." He closed the small space between them and extracted a kiss. His body temperature rocketed as he swallowed her moan and pulled her closer.

Ryan couldn't believe how good she tasted, how soft she felt. A part of him wanted to analyze what she was doing to him, the other part wanted to get lost in the moment.

Thick, massive clouds of confusion filled Joey's head, while her mind and body were out of sync. She loved Laurence, so why was she kissing some sleazy director? Well, maybe not sleazy…sex-starved?

Then again, it was hard not to kiss him, and harder still to stop kissing him. His lips were like nice soft pillows and he had a way of setting her body on fire.

His tongue delved into her mouth and stole her breath. Impulsively she wrapped her arms around his neck and clung for dear life.

Suddenly she had a moment of clarity. If she went through with this, she could be making the biggest mistake of her life. She loved Laurence, so why was she allowing this sex-starved director to untie her robe?

She needed this, she argued back. She needed the comfort he offered. It didn't matter that he was using her. She was using him, too. Didn't that make everything all right?

Ryan peeled the robe from her shoulders and then broke their kiss so he could gaze down at her naked body. "Perfect," he whispered.

His words brought another rush of tears to her eyes. Laurence never looked this adoringly at her, and he certainly never declared her "perfect."

"Hey, what are these for?" He kissed away her tears and cupped her breasts. They filled his hands completely, and she held her breath as his head descended lower. At the slight flicker of his tongue across her taut nipple, she shivered and arched her back to give him better access.

Ryan chuckled, flicked his tongue again and was rewarded with another soft moan. He slid out of his robe. *Yes. I'm back in the game.*

The moment the thought crossed his mind, Joey firmly pushed at his chest and ended his tender suckling.

Her eyes roamed over him. Judging by the muscles and the chiseled contours, he was an athlete. He suddenly exuded a strength she hadn't noticed before. "You're perfect, too," she said and meant it.

A small smile curved his lips. "I'm glad to hear the lady is pleased." His fingers lazily circled the dark centers of her breasts before he bent his head low for another taste.

"I hardly know you," she said in between heavy pants.

"My name is Ryan Scott Donovan. Born and raised in Los Angeles. I'm forty-five, drug and disease free, and I earn a pretty decent living directing movies." He pulled her back to him and refilled his greedy mouth with her succulent breast.

"What…what about me?" she asked.

"I know all I need to know," he mumbled shifting to the other breast. His body ached and throbbed in a way that was foreign to him.

Joey roamed her hands through his short-cropped hair and then held him steady while he sucked, licked and tugged at her nipple.

Gently, he eased her back until she lay flat against the blanket. His patience strained while he struggled to pace himself. She felt tiny beneath his large hands, but he loved her slight curves and thick bottom.

Pressing his knees between her thighs, Ryan smiled when she willingly opened her legs for him.

"But I love…Laurence," she whispered.

"I know. I know. I just want to make you feel good." He dipped his finger inside of her, pleased to find her slick and ready. "Don't you want to feel good?" He slid in another finger.

Vigorously Joey nodded while her chest rose and fell as though she raced a marathon.

"Good, then we're on the same page," he whispered as his fingers stroked her smooth and steady.

Joey's deep moans caught in her throat, and then transformed into begging whimpers. She still didn't know what the hell she was doing and why she was enjoying it, but she did know she didn't want him to stop. This was just a one-night fling. It didn't mean anything.

Ryan had no plans to stop. He knew what she wanted—what she needed, but currently he was caught up in his game of cat and mouse. His strokes slowed and he watched in pure delight as she wiggled her rump to urge him on.

"Please," she begged.

"Please what?" He nuzzled her neck and drew the thin flesh in between his teeth.

"Please," she continued, seemingly unable to say much more.

"Is this what you want?" Ryan deepened and quickened his stokes. "Hmm?"

She tried to speak, but no words came.

He slowed down. "I can't hear you?"

She bounced her body against his hand, blending his name with, "Y-yes!"

Her body's honey flowed freely as her legs trembled around his hand. Ryan's mouth returned to her marble-hard nipples and less than a second later her body trembled violently with her orgasm.

Refusing to stop, Ryan slid in his thumb and gently massaged her swollen nub.

Joey's hips came off the floor and she squirmed to get away from him, however, he dogged her every inch. Before she could catch her breath another body quake erupted and left her writhing beneath him.

He was ready to clinch the deal when she stopped him.

"Not here," she said softly as tears crested her eyes. Her hand glided lazily down his face. "Take me to the bed."

Her dark lusty gaze trapped his own. "You got it." He climbed off her.

She smiled as he slid his arms beneath her. No words were necessary as he carried her toward the main bedroom. When he reached the king-size bed, he laid her down and was unable to pull his gaze away.

She really was perfect.

Joey curled onto her side and smiled. "You have any protection?"

Ryan snapped back to his senses and remembered the condoms in the other room. "Don't go away. I'll be right back." He sprinted out and raced to the fireplace. "Thank you, thank you, thank you," he praised and dug the two condoms out of his wallet and sprinted back. He was certain he'd made an Olympic track record to the bedroom.

"I'm back," he sang, easing up to the bed.

Joey remained curled in the same position he'd left her, yet she was fast asleep.

"Joey?" He sat down next to her and gently rocked her shoulders. "Joey?"

She didn't move but emitted a soft snore.

He continued to shake her. "No, no. This can't be happening."

Unfortunately, it was.

Chapter 16

The Adams family argued nonstop over who all should head out to Italy. Sheldon regretfully backed out because of her budding tribe of rug rats.

Marlin didn't see the point. "Joseph is a grown woman and is more than capable of taking care of herself."

To show exactly what she thought of that statement, Michael twirled a finger at her temple and waved off her father. "Joseph is emotional. The only thing she is going to do is make a fool out herself in front of a man who doesn't want her. She should just cut her losses."

"Is this the same woman who browbeat, hog-tied and dragged her man kicking and screaming to the altar?" Peyton joked.

"The last thing I want is for Joey to make the same mistake I made."

Everyone's eyes darted to one another, but no one spoke.

"I'm definitely going," Michael added, not noticing the room's sudden silence.

"Count me in," Frankie said.

Flex folded his arms. "I've never been to Italy."

The girls' heads swiveled in surprise in his direction.

"Don't you have to go back to Georgia?" Lincoln asked. "What about your job?"

"I still have a week left of vacation. How long will it take to club Joey over the head and drag her back home?"

Peyton turned her inquiring eyes toward her husband.

"What?" He frowned. "The house is finally finished." He inched closer as he lowered his voice. "We haven't finished christening the rooms."

A few snickers rippled around them; but when Lincoln glanced back, everyone managed to straighten their faces.

Peyton pressed her body against him and encircled her arms around his neck. "You know, we could treat it like a second honeymoon."

"We?" He blinked. "I have an art show to get ready for. I can't just take off to Italy."

"Then if you're going to be busy, you'll hardly notice I'm gone."

"You're going to go to Italy without me?"

Sheldon, Frankie, and Michael glanced at each other and shook their heads.

"I'm sure you're going to be just fine without me." Peyton patted his chest reassuringly. "Just no wild parties while I'm gone." She leaned up on her toes and planted a kiss against his cheek. "But when I get back…anything goes." She winked.

"P.J., I'm still in the room," Marlin mumbled under his breath.

For the first time since Joey's disappearance, the close-knit family erupted with laughter.

Joey slept like a baby.

After two days of sleeping on hard benches or curled up against cold stone, her body surrendered to the bed's plush, downy softness and her mind just drifted away.

Shifting against the pillow, her face was suddenly bathed in rich sunlight. She stretched and moaned, and then moaned and stretched; she didn't care to open her eyes. In fact, she had no desire to leave her safe cocoon anytime soon until…

"Welcome to the land of the living."

Ryan's honey-coated baritone oozed into her head and elicited a soft smile, but she still made no effort to get up.

"Please tell me you don't intend to lie there all day."

"And what if I do?" she asked, finally peeking from behind her mesh of long lashes. "Are you going to have hotel security throw me out?"

"Now there's a novel idea." He crammed a cigar into his mouth.

Joey picked up on his irritation, but she refused to be baited by it. She felt too damn good, and frankly he was still looking pretty good in his robe. Her smile evaporated. *What am I thinking?*

Slowly she pushed herself up on the pillows. When she did so, the sheet slipped and exposed her apple-size breasts, but she quickly retrieved it.

"Are we suddenly modest this morning?"

"N-no." She flustered. "It's just—"

"Things change with the light of day," he finished for her. His eyes were hard and challenging.

She was the first to lower her eyes. "I'm sorry I fell asleep on you."

"Are you?" He walked toward the foot of the bed and sat down.

Though she didn't look up, the weight of his stare dragged her shoulders down a few more notches. "Maybe I wasn't thinking clearly."

"But you are now?"

"Yes."

"And you're still in love with this Larry character?" His voice tightened, but she couldn't tell whether it was with anger or annoyance.

"Yes." To her surprise, he laughed. Joey glanced up. "What's so funny?"

"You are." He stood and continued laughing. "I guess it's just human nature to want the things we can't have. It seems I have the same dysfunction. His eyes pierced her, and she quickly understood his meaning.

"But you don't know me." She clutched the sheet tighter.

"Calm down. I'm not looking for a lifetime commitment." He snickered, shaking his head. "I'm thinking along the same lines you were last night."

"A one-night stand?"

"Well, one that doesn't include snoring." He winked and zapped the seriousness out of his tone.

Joey's smile returned. "Sorry about that. Did I keep you up?"

"Nah. I slept in the other room after a long—very long—cold shower." He slid his hands into his robe and mumbled, "So much for ending my dry spell."

If nothing, Joey had perfect hearing. "What dry spell?"

Ryan blinked, realizing what he'd said aloud. He quickly became flustered. "Uh, well. Nothing. It's nothing." He couldn't help it, but he squirmed beneath her stare. "Room service is bringing up breakfast. I'll let you get dressed."

"Wait." Joey scrambled to climb off the large bed, while gathering and wrapping the bedding's top sheet around her body.

It didn't completely work; Ryan caught a flash of her left butt cheek as she stood up.

"There's something you're not telling me."

Hoping to avoid interrogation, Ryan turned and strolled toward the door. Though her legs weren't as long as his, she managed to catch up with him before he crossed the threshold.

"C'mon." She caught him by the arm. "Give. I told you everything. Why are you holding out? What dry spell?"

"It's nothing," Ryan said again. His eyes didn't quite meet hers.

Joey laughed as she guessed. "Don't tell me a well-to-do director like you hasn't had sex in a while?"

"No…it's not like that. I mean…"

"Models, actresses, groupies—the world is your oyster," she reasoned, but her gaze kept him under tight scrutiny. "No. You wouldn't have a problem *getting* a date. So that leaves…"

"It leaves nothing." He pulled back his arm and then immediately sighed with relief at the light tap at the door. "Ah, breakfast. I don't know about you but I'm starving!" He sprinted toward the door.

Joey wasn't fooled.

Ryan opened the door and greeted room service with a boisterous hello and literally became as animated as a cartoon character as he gestured their stunned waiter into the room.

"Ah, everything smells delicious." Ryan dramatically inhaled the breakfast aroma and glanced back over to her. "Heavenly, don't you think?"

"Heavenly," Joey echoed as she continued to clutch the sheet around her body and leaned against the bedroom's door frame.

With his smile still too wide to fit his face, Ryan produced a money clip seemingly from thin air and tipped their waiter.

Joey just watched and waited until they were alone.

"Care to join me?" he asked, once the suite's door closed.

She crossed the room with her own smile widening. "Sooo. Have you thought about Viagra?"

"No," he lied forcefully. "Because there is nothing wrong." He straightened his shoulders. "It's true that I've been under a great deal of stress—but that is all. You know, I was at full salute last night."

Her brows dipped dubiously. "Me thinks thou dost protest too much." She inched closer to him. "How long has this dry spell been exactly?"

"I'm through talking about this." He lifted a silver lid off their breakfast to reveal his requested fluffy buttermilk pancakes.

Joey closed in until there was barely an inch separating them. Enjoying a power she'd never experienced before, she slowly walked her fingers up his arm. "Sooo...last night, was that the first time you were at, ah, full salute in say, two months? Three months?"

Though his thick terry-cloth robe covered his arms, Ryan's body still reacted to her touch as though they were still cuddled together before the fireplace.

"Four months?" she continued to guess.

What harm will it be to tell her the truth? Ryan asked himself. Maybe if he were honest, she would break him off a little somethin'-somethin'.

"Six months?" she asked, amusement seeping into her voice. "Surely no longer than that?"

"Actually, Ms. Adams." He turned toward her, attempting to mask his embarrassment. "It's not important how *long* I've had my little problem but only that it seems to go away every time you're around." His hungry eyes feasted on her ethereal beauty.

Despite the fact he hadn't made love to her last night, she still wore that sexy, mussed-up look that begged him to sweep her into his arms and carry her back off to bed, Rhett Butler style.

As Joey stared up into Ryan's gorgeous eyes, her body's alarm system went haywire. Her knees weakened, every limb tingled and her breasts hardened like marbles.

"What about you?" he asked suddenly.

"Me?" she croaked, and then licked her dry lips. "What about me?"

"Do I affect you in any way?"

She swallowed thickly, but the frog in her throat refused to budge. "N-no."

Ryan's eyebrows knitted close together. "That's funny because last night—"

"I had too much to drink."

"You only had one glass—"

"I have a low tolerance."

"You didn't even finish—"

"Look, Mr. Donovan," she stressed, as her smile turned plastic. "I admit last night I was feeling a little vulnerable and you were saying all the right things." Joey drew a deep breath. "But the fact of the matter is that I'm still in love with Larry—I mean, Laurence. He's the one I want…not you."

Doubt telegraphed across his handsome features. "Now who doth protest too much?"

For a few seconds Joey couldn't volley a smart comeback. Instead she swirled on her heel and marched back to the bedroom—completely forgetting that her butt was still exposed.

While standing at full salute, Ryan had never seen a more glorious moon than the one that was storming away from him now.

Chapter 17

Laurence feared he'd made the biggest mistake of his life. Why else was he seeing Joey's face everywhere he and Carlina traveled? Sometimes she was a face in a crowd or a woman racing by a store's front window. And honest to goodness, one time she was a pair eyes peering at them through some shrubbery at the hotel.

With his wedding looming, he wondered if these wild imaginings weren't his mind's way of telling him something. Or perhaps he was just simply suffering from cold feet.

Laurence took another sip of his morning coffee and flipped open the last Hollywood tabloid paper that Carlina had requested to be specially delivered to her door. And just as they had hoped there was picture of them on the front page with the caption: Carlina Takes a Groom?

Laurence turned the picture this way and that, a little annoyed that the photographer had snapped his bad side. It wasn't the first time his name had appeared in the tabloids—a few celebrity patients praised his work here and there—but this was the first time his picture was splashed across a major publication.

He liked it. No, he *loved* it.

He'd landed the perfect trophy wife. And soon, being married to Hollywood's "it" girl was going to rake him in some serious Benjamins at the office.

Sighing, he smiled in contentment. Yet, seconds later, Joey reemerged from the back of his mind. In hindsight, maybe he should have kept her as his mistress. He closed the paper.

Maybe it's not too late.

Sitting outside on the presidential suite's terrace, Ryan swallowed the last of his morning coffee while stealing coveted glances at his "guest." She sat demurely across from him doing a lousy job at pretending he wasn't there.

The hotel had cleaned her jeans and underwear, but had been unsuccessful in removing the questionable stains in her T-shirt. As a solution, Ryan volunteered one of his shirts. Why did he do that? There was nothing sexier to a man than to have a woman wearing his clothes.

"I've been thinking," he said out of the blue.

Joey glanced up but eyed him suspiciously. "Should I call someone? The media perhaps?"

"Very funny." He leaned back in his chair and studied her. "I think I'm going to help you win your Larry back."

"Laurence."

"Whatever." He waved off the correction. "It's clear to me that planning isn't one of your strongest attributes so I'm going to help you," he announced triumphantly and then waited as if he expected her to shower him with gratitude.

"Why would you want to help me?"

"Why not?" he retorted with a shrug. "I'd like to think that we've become pretty good friends in the past week, wouldn't you say?"

"No."

His face collapsed in calculated disappointment. "You wound me."

"And you insult my intelligence." She crossed her arms. "I say that makes us about even."

"Even? Haven't I proven myself trustworthy by now? I've rescued you from a men's restroom window, whisked you away from VIP, punched your fiancé out for humiliating you—"

"You punched Laurence?"

"No need to thank me. Where was I? Oh. I rescued you from the streets of Milan, fed you, let you have a hot shower, had one serious bout of foreplay and provided shelter. I say, what's *one* more favor?"

Joey shifted in her chair. "Well, when you put it like that."

"Is there any other way to put it?"

Drawing a deep breath, she thought it over. "What's your plan?"

"We play his game."

"What game?" she asked, crossing her arms. "Larry—Laurence isn't into head games."

Ryan's head rocked back with laughter. "You're kidding me, right? Everyone plays head games. It's part of the chase."

She straightened in her chair. "*I* don't play head games."

Ryan pinned her with a look.

"Much," she added.

"And last night?"

"I told you, I had too much to drink," she declared, her neck heated with embarrassment.

"Right. Right. I remember now." He rolled his eyes and retrieved a new cigar.

"How can you stand those things?" She shook her head in disgust.

"These little babies—" he chuckled as he gazed lovingly at the thick cigars "—are better than sex."

"Spoken like a man who hasn't had sex in what— eight months?" She winked.

"It certainly hasn't been for lack of trying," he conceded. "In fact, I'm willing to bet that after I help you win poor Larry—"

"Laurence."

"Whatever. My bet is, when he's groveling at your feet, wanting you to take him back, you won't want him."

Joey laughed and folded her arms against the late-morning chill. "Okay. I'll bite. Why wouldn't I want him back?"

"Because you'll want me," he answered with a straight face.

"Come again?"

"What part did you miss?"

"The part where you banged your head—on something hard."

"It's a harmless bet." He shrugged. "If I lose, you get your darling *Laurence* back, and if I win, I get you."

She laughed again but her stomach fluttered with nervous butterflies. Judging by the intensity of his dark gaze, Joey concluded Ryan was serious. The crazy part— she was actually thinking about taking him up on his offer.

After all, what did she have to lose?

"And you think you can actually help me win Laurence back?"

"Absolutely."

"How?"

"Do we have a deal?"

His cockiness worried her, but logic contradicted his claim. There was no way she would ever *want* him. Well, last night she wanted him—but she would never want him the way she wanted Larry…Laurence. That much she was certain. "All right. You have yourself a deal."

The Adamses minus Sheldon and Marlin had no problem discovering where to start looking for their emotionally charged sibling. Thanks to a front-page splash on a cheesy tabloid newspaper.

Carlina Takes a Groom.

"He's engaged to an actress?" Frankie said. "Does Joey know this?"

"She knows," Michael confirmed, shaking her head at the picture. "That really is his bad side."

"How come you know more about this than we do?" Peyton accused. "The last I heard, he dumped her on

Valentine's Day. Joey said nothing about him marrying someone—oh."

"What?" Frankie stomped her foot. "You know something, too."

"Well." Peyton lowered her voice as they paid for the paper and walked away from the airport newsstand. "Joey said that she found a receipt for a ring. An expensive ring. Goes to say that if he didn't present it to her, then—"

"He gave it the world's most overexposed actress," Frankie concluded. "Poor Joey."

"If she knows he's engaged why did she fly—the voice message." Peyton snapped her finger. "He said that he was confused and that he still loved her."

"Oh, he's good," Michael marveled. "I can't wait until he goes home."

"Okay. Now you're just not making any sense," Frankie said as they rejoined Flex at their gate.

"Well." A sinister smile slithered across Michael's raspberry-tinted lips. "I, sort of, helped Joey with a little revenge last week at the *good* doctor's residence."

"You didn't!" The small family clan chimed.

"I did," Michael assured them triumphantly. "Joey was at home sobbing her eyes out and overdosing on ice cream when she called me. So—" she shrugged "—I helped her."

"And what happened?" Peyton braced herself for the worst.

"We were arrested."

"What?" They all thundered.

The group gasped and stared openmouthed at her.

"It was all worth it, if you ask me. You don't mess with an Adams!"

"You need psychiatric help," Flex said, shaking his head. "I've always said that."

"Whatever." Michael waved him off. "She asked for help and I helped her. And here we are again—helping her."

He nodded and then slipped into a brief reverie. "You know, I think I've changed my mind about this."

"What?" The girls turned toward him.

Flex chuckled under his breath and slipped his carry-on bag over his shoulder. "If I go through with this then I'm just part of the madness. Dad is right. Joseph is a grown woman more than capable of handling her own problems."

Michael's face blazed with incredulity. "So you're just going to stand back and let her mess up her life?"

"The point is—it's *her* life." He stepped toward Michael and probed her heated gaze. "You know I'll do anything for you girls. Anything legal. If Joey wanted our help, she knows how to ask for it. And that goes for you, too. If you want to talk about it, I'm here." With that, he strolled away from the gate.

His sisters watched his departure with open mouths.

"Can you *believe* him?" Michael hissed incredulously. When Frankie and Peyton didn't answer, her neck swiveled in their direction. "Well?"

"Actually, I think he has a point," Peyton croaked, and then shifted on her feet.

"It is *Joey's* life," Frankie acquiesced. "She should be free to make her own mistakes."

"What?" Michael stared at them as though she'd never seen them before.

"C'mon, Mike," Peyton pleaded. "The girl is thirty-five going on eighteen the way we baby her—and she's not even the baby. Look how much damage we did with Francis last year."

"We? Francis brought that crap down on himself when he lied about dating your husband."

"But you were the one who ambushed him with a reunion with Morgan," Frankie said.

"Hey, hey." Peyton noticed the weird stares they were getting. "Lower your voices." When her sisters settled down, Peyton also slung her carry-on bag over her shoulder. "I've changed my mind."

Frankie picked up her bag. "Me, too."

"Whoa. Whoa." Michael panicked at being ousted as ringleader. "Just yesterday you guys thought this was a great idea."

"It was," Frankie attempted to placate Michael's ire. "But today, this is a better idea. We know Joey went to Italy. We all have a feeling on how this is going to turn out. If we go rescue her with our capes billowing in the wind, there is a good chance Joey will resent us."

"Sort of like I did after I divorced Ricky," Peyton said.

"You got over it," Michael chirped with a shrug.

"Not really," Peyton said honestly. "Yes you told me not to marry Ricky, yes, you kept telling me how 'no good' he was while I was married, and yes, you chanted, 'I told you so' after the divorce. But it shouldn't have gone down like that."

"You're making it sound like *I'm* the bad guy here."

"No, I'm just saying it's time we learned from our mistakes. Let Joey do what she has to do. If it turns out badly, let's just be her shoulder to cry on—if that's what she needs." When Michael failed to respond, Peyton hugged her and walked away.

Frankie followed suit.

"Continental Airlines is now boarding flight 886 for Milan, Italy, at gate sixty-five."

Alone, Michael groaned and plopped down into a hard, plastic chair. Tears brimmed before she had a chance to think to stop them. Her mutinous siblings had deserted her—just as her husband had six months ago.

Michael cupped her face in her hands and wept.

Chapter 18

Zach had heard some wild things in his lifetime, but as he sat listening to his buddy, Ryan, in the director's chair, he was certain that he'd finally heard it all. "That makes absolutely no sense," he declared.

Ryan chuckled good-naturedly and turned his gaze to watch the stage crew work their magic on a quaint Milan villa. "Trust me. I know what I'm doing."

"You're not on some kind of drugs, are you?"

"Zach—"

"I mean, you could tell me if you were. I know how to keep a secret."

"No drugs." He smiled. "I'm just a man on a mission."

"But why?" Zach frowned, thinking of the woman Ryan dragged in from the streets. "Seems like an awful lot trouble for…that type of girl."

Ryan's smile quickly turned into a scowl. "And what type is that?"

Zach shrugged but didn't know how else to say it, "The ordinary type—the dirty, ordinary type."

In a flash Ryan's smile and good humor returned. "Believe me. She cleans up good."

Zach had a hard time imagining that. "Whatever, man. I guess I should be happy to see you back in the game. Like I said, I was worried about you, there, for a minute."

"Mr. Donovan?"

Ryan turned to his new set assistant, Belladonna Capri.

"The team is ready for the storyboard meeting," she informed him.

"Right. I'm on my way." He stood from his chair, but turned toward Zach. "Do me a favor. Carlina and her new fiancé are staying at our hotel. See if you can finesse the concierge into telling you where their dinner plans are and then book reservations for Joey and me. You might even want to get yourself a table. You don't want to miss the fireworks I have planned for this evening."

Zach eyed his friend with measured curiosity. "All right. I like a good show as well as the next guy. I'll see what I can do." He turned to leave.

"Oh, wait." Ryan stopped him. "There's one more thing."

Joey felt as though she was living someone else's life. Part one of Ryan's mysterious plan, the only part he'd told her about, was for her to buy some new clothes. Penniless but proud, Joey protested the suggestion because there was no way she could afford to pay him back. She was already indebted to Frankie for the airline ticket, not counting that she still needed to find a way to pay for a ticket home.

Yet Ryan quickly pointed out that she couldn't think to woo Laurence back in her present and only attire. She reluctantly agreed to the new clothes. However, she was unprepared when a personal shopper was appointed to her and a slew of clothes was delivered to the presidential suite. There were some designers she recognized from Frankie's closet and some she had only read about in fashion magazines.

Ryan was spending a fortune, and Joey was feeling nauseous.

Sergio, her personal shopper, pretended or refused to tell her how much anything cost so she did the only thing she could think of: pretend not to like anything. Of course that only worked until Sergio divulged a small tidbit.

"That dress looks so much better on you than Carlina Leoni."

Joey froze as she stared at her reflection. The white floor-length gown was adorned with beaded crystals around the collar and waist. The only flaw was that there was no back to the damn thing. She could catch her death in it.

"Carlina bought this dress?"

"No. No," he said in an accent nearly too thick to understand. "She wanted to, but with those bodacious tatas…" He smiled. "Let's just say not everyone can wear Prada."

She twirled before the mirror again, this time

paying particular attention to how elegantly the dress hugged her body.

"I know for a fact if Carlina was to see you in this dress, she would be green with envy," he added, and clinched the sale.

"I'll take it," Joey announced. Once she bought one dress it was easier for her to buy another one—and then another one. Before she knew it, she and Sergio had selected a full wardrobe.

However, Ryan had a few more surprises up his sleeves.

When the first batch of tall, brawny men dressed in what could only be described as FBI blues arrived, Joey feared the hotel was about to escort her off the premises. Instead the men proceeded to open suitcases filled with priceless gems.

"Your...boyfriend," Sergio whispered, "has spared no expense. You must make him very happy."

Joey's hand floated up to her mouth. "I...I have done no such thing," she admitted. Caving in to temptation, she leaned over one suitcase and ogled a choker with four rows of round-cut diamonds.

Sergio chuckled and elbowed her. "Don't just stare at it. Try it on."

She shook her head, fearful to even touch the thing. "How many total carats you think it is?"

Sergio reached for the glittering gem and read a tiny card attached. "Eighty carats."

Joey took a retreating step. "Is he crazy?"

"A good kind of crazy, no?"

"I'm not wearing that thing. What if I break it or lose it?"

"You'll do no such thing," he assured. "Besides I'm sure it's insured. Now turn around."

Despite her racing heart, she did as her shopper instructed and still gasped when the beautiful necklace descended before her eyes and finally came to rest around her long neck.

Both she and Sergio stared at her reflection.

She wore only her simple jeans and Ryan's business shirt, nothing special had been done to her hair and her face bore no makeup. In spite of that, Joey hardly recognized the woman in the mirror.

There was something about the magnificent piece that transformed her instantly. She wasn't simple or tomboyish, but lithe and elegant.

"This was made for you," Sergio whispered.

For one crazy moment Joey believed him. "I'll take it."

"Great. Now let's find some earrings."

Usually a devoted workaholic, Ryan surprised everyone by ending their first official workday early. Immediately afterward his cell vibrated against his hip and the *very* concerned producers of *La Bella Vida* questioned whether there was a problem.

"Al, trust me," he said, sliding into his limousine. "I have everything under control. The crew will continue working on the set tomorrow morning and the starring cast will meet for their first read-through at the hotel's conference room. Shooting is still set for the day after tomorrow." He bobbed his head and half listened to his caller.

"Right, right. You're not losing any money," he said

the magic phrase and quickly ended the call. "Did you make the reservations?"

On the other side of the limousine, Zach sighed and folded his arms. "I made your reservations at the hotel's Galleria."

"Great." His smile radiated as he clapped his hands together. "What about the other thing I asked you?"

Zach drew a heavy breath and shook his head at his friend. "I have to ask you this again. Are you sure you know what you're doing?"

"Positive." Ryan winked. He hadn't felt this giddy since his first movie premier.

Zach stared. When Ryan continued to smile, Zach reached into his coat pocket and handed over his afternoon task. "Just remember, I warned you against this."

Carlina Leoni had only ever had one ambition in life: to be the most famous actress in the world. Despite her latest stinker-slash-box-office-hit, she was still on course. As she soaked in a luxurious milk bath, she stared at the latest tabloid newspaper, pleased to have snatched the front page.

As she opened the magazine and perused through its glossy pages, she realized that her engagement to a brilliant plastic surgeon didn't qualify them as a red-carpet power couple.

With the likes of Tom Cruise and Nicole Kidman, Brad Pitt and Jennifer Aniston, and even the infamous Ben Affleck and Jennifer Lopez dismembered, Hollywood was in desperate need of the next golden couple.

Carlina sighed and leaned her head back against her inflated seashell bath pillow and pondered whether she'd made a mistake. At the age of twenty-five, she was already overdue for her first *start-up* marriage.

Maybe she should have pulled a Britney Spears weekend-wedding special with Larry instead of a rushed Italian getaway during a movie shoot like her agent had suggested.

Of course, after the divorce her heartbreak would be splashed over every magazine cover. If lucky, she would even get a CNN news scroll announcing the split à la Bennifer and gain some much-needed sympathy points.

There were just so many career decisions to be made. Like how long should she stay married—a weekend, a month, three months?

Six months was out of the question.

Larry's constant quest for perfection was already getting on her nerves. Not to mention, it took everything she had not to scratch his eyes out for calling her Jo-Jo in bed.

Carlina remembered Larry's ex-girlfriend from the Blue Diamond and still felt a sliver of jealousy for the woman's effortless beauty. Larry's Jo-Jo was what many people in the industry called a "natural beauty." She didn't have to inject foreign objects or plaster on expensive makeup to get noticed.

Who didn't hate women like that? Carlina's only concern was *what* Jo-Jo was doing at the Blue Diamond with Ryan. Because when this was all over, Carlina wanted to move in for the kill on the real man she wanted for a husband.

A man powerful enough to keep her in the Holly-wood game long after her youth and beauty began to fade. Say when she hit thirty or something. The man she'd purposely followed from picture to picture: Hollywood director Ryan Donovan.

Chapter 19

Ryan waltzed into his hotel suite anxious to see Joey at the end of a long day. He looked forward to showing her a great time and showing her off. More than once his mind wandered with thoughts of her—some of them were erotic, most were not.

He was fascinated by more than just his physical reaction; he liked the sound of her laughter. It was lyrical and infectious. Ryan even liked her childlike impulsiveness. But, more important, Joey was a woman in love with love.

Dr. Benson had been a lucky man and he didn't even know it.

"Lucy, I'm home." Ryan called out in his best Ricky Ricardo voice as his long strides carried him across the spacious suite. From one of the bedrooms he heard the spray of water and followed its sound.

He opened the right bedroom door and called, "Joey?"

The shower shut off in the adjoining bathroom.

"Ryan?" she shouted back.

"Yeah, it's me." He smiled at the casual intimacy already established between them and admitted to himself that he liked it.

"You're early!" Joey grabbed a towel and stepped out of the shower. She wrapped it around her and rushed to the bathroom door and peeked out. "I'm not ready."

"You have plenty of time. I'm going to jump in the shower myself before we head out."

"What...in here?" she asked, though she already knew the answer, but given her mood, she couldn't stop herself from flirting.

Smiling, he approached the bathroom. "Is that an invitation I hear?" He caught a glimpse of her bare shoulder and could feel another salute in the works. Joey continued to have quite an effect on him.

"Are you kidding me? If I broke you off a piece, I'll never be able to get rid of you."

Ryan laughed. "I won't be the only one whipped."

Her laughter danced around him as he leaned against the door frame. "So how was your shopping today?"

"Surprising, unexpected and way over the top."

"But you liked it?"

"I had a nice time."

"Good. Then you'll have an even better time tonight." He leaned forward to sneak a more-revealing peek at her.

"Hey!" She slammed the door but continued to laugh. "Go get dressed," Joey directed.

"Yes, ma'am," he thundered like an army private, and then marched off into another bedroom to carry out the order.

Joey listened as his heavy footfall padded out of the room. When she glanced up at the vanity mirror, she caught the smile still on her lips. "Do you have any idea what you're doing?" she asked herself for what seemed like the millionth time.

Slowly she lowered her gaze and pretended not to hear the small voice in her head when it answered, "No."

An hour later Ryan rechecked his appearance in the full-length mirror in his bedroom. He had prepared for more than a thousand red-carpet events and award shows and never had he worried more about his appearance than he did at that moment.

At heart, he was a jeans and football jersey kind of man; let it never be said that Ryan Donovan didn't know how to flip the script. Tonight's special, a double-breasted black Armani, fit his body like a glove, and he grew more anxious to drape the ultimate male accessory on his arm: a beautiful woman.

"Joey," he called, stepping out of his bedroom. "Are you about ready?" He headed toward the bar to prepare drinks.

The last thing Ryan expected was for a woman to be on time, but that was exactly what happened when Joey's bedroom door crept open. He pivoted in its direction, his breath trapped in his chest.

He had expected her to be beautiful, but in truth she was more than that. Stunning, striking, gorgeous—no one word encompassed the vision that floated toward him in a floor-length white gown with something that looked like stars glittering around her arms and waist. To complete the look, diamonds sparkled around her lean, elegant neck and even dripped from her ears.

"Aren't you going to say something?"

Ryan's eyebrows stretched higher and his jaw slackened, but words continued to fail him.

"You don't like it," she said. Her shoulders immediately drooped. "I knew it was too much." Joey turned, flashing her flawless back. "I better go change. Just give me a few minutes."

"Don't you dare." His voice returned full force.

Slowly she faced him.

"Don't you change a thing." Ryan walked toward her. "You are perfect."

She cocked her head as though concerned with his mental state.

"You don't know, do you?" he asked, closing the distance between them in two easy strides. "You don't know how truly beautiful you are."

Joey rolled her eyes. "I'm no Carlina Leoni."

He shrugged. "You're right." Her gaze lowered to the carpet, but Ryan settled his finger beneath her chin and lifted her head so that their eyes would meet. "You're better than her. You're real."

Her clear, chocolate-colored eyes glossed with unshed tears. They widened briefly as they watched his head descend, but then closed a split second before his pillow-soft lips landed on hers.

She was getting used to the taste of him and could feel herself becoming addicted. That made no sense. She was in love with…what was his name?

Unable to think straight, Joey wondered why she felt as if her body grew lighter, weightless—as though floating on a cloud. His lips pulled away, but she greedily leaned forward to recapture them and prolong their kiss.

At last it was Ryan's soft chuckle that burst her languid reverie, and she jumped back, completely baffled with what she'd just did.

"No need to look like that. I enjoyed it, too." He winked and turned back toward the bar. "Would you like a drink before we go downstairs for dinner?"

Still stunned into silence, Joey lifted her slender hand to her lips. What was wrong with her? She was behaving like a fickle teenager who developed crushes on a new boy every week.

"Joey?" he called, setting two glasses on the bar. "Do you like Cristal?"

"S-sure." She pushed out the solitary word, and then cleared her throat when she realized that she sounded like Kermit the Frog.

Ryan smiled.

"So." She composed herself and joined him at the bar. "What is the next step in your master plan? Surely there is more to it than a hostile makeover."

"Hostile?"

She bit her lower lip. "Forced?"

His brows dipped and collided together. "Sergio held a gun to your head, did he?"

Her gaze dropped. "Fine. A *fun* makeover."

Ryan's smile returned. "Yes, there is more to my plan." He filled their glasses. "Joey, did you know that men are *very* simple creatures—animals, actually?"

Her lips sloped into an uneven smile. "I've heard rumors."

"It's true." Ryan handed her a glass. "Simple. Primitive. Even in the twenty-first century when we don expensive Armani suits, drive fast cars and drip diamonds over our prey…"

Joey shifted nervously on her feet and sipped her drink.

"…a man is still a hunter. We live for the hunt, the thrill of the chase." Ryan clinked his glass against hers. "A man wants the very thing he thinks he can't have." He took the first sip of his drink.

"Okay," she said slowly, but still looked confused.

"When Larry—"

"Laurence."

Ryan exhaled impatiently. "When *Laurence* sees you tonight, he will see a magnificent creature, undoubtedly the most beautiful woman in the room. You will be happy, exuberant, and you will act as though you're completely over him."

"What?"

"This is a very important part of the plan," he said, and took another sip. "Because another unfortunate male truth is—men view the woman they've been with as marked territory."

"That's absurd!"

"Yes, but it's true. It's vital for a man to feel that he can return to the arms of any woman of his past."

"But he broke up with me," she said indignantly.

"Doesn't matter. If Dr. Benson sees you happy with another man—especially so soon after the breakup— he will become obsessed with trying to prove to himself that he can still have you. And you will behave as though he can't." Ryan watched her and finished his drink while his words sank into her head.

"So, all I have to do is just laugh?" she asked, lifting her beautiful eyes up at him.

"That…and pretend that I'm the most important man in your life."

Her brows rose in suspicion.

"Think about what I said," Ryan reminded her. "He views you as his property so—"

"He doesn't want to see another man with his property?" she asked, catching on.

"Exactly." His chest filled with triumph. "Do you think you can do it? Do you think that you can pretend to make me the center of your universe?"

"Well, I'm no actress." She shrugged. "Speaking of which…what will Carlina be doing while Laurence is fawning over me?"

"Don't worry about her."

"How can I not?"

"I'll take care of Ms. Leoni."

Joey's face, once again, twisted in confusion. "How?"

"Well, let's just say that it's time for me to see if I can salute another woman."

"Oh." She blinked, startled by a stab of jealousy. "Oh, so you think your…little problem—"

"Shouldn't be such a problem." A wicked smile slithered across his face. "I've been feeling pretty good lately."

"Well, I wouldn't want you…want you to do that just for me. I mean, that's a little above the call of duty, don't you think?"

"Ah, well. It's a favor I don't mind doing."

"I see." Joey took a deep breath and drained the rest of her champagne.

Ryan chuckled. "Don't forget your low tolerance."

"I think I might need another." Her gaze darted around and seemed to have trouble landing on him.

"I think you should wait until dinner." He winked and offered his arm. "I think it's better for you to glide into the restaurant instead of stumble."

Joey nodded and fluttered a smile, even though her stomach twisted into knots.

"Oh, wait a minute," Ryan said, and reached into his jacket pocket. "I forgot to give you this." He withdrew a small jewelry box and popped it open.

Joey gasped at the sight of the most beautiful diamond ring she'd ever laid eyes on. "Wh-what's this?"

"Your engagement ring." Ryan shrugged, but his hands trembled slightly. "I had a friend of mine purchase it for me this afternoon. He did a good job, don't you think?"

The only thing that crossed Joey's mind was that she would have to wear sunglasses to wear a diamond that big. "Ryan, I don't know. I think it's…too much."

"A ring is important…for our charade."

Their eyes locked as Ryan removed the ring from the box and slid it up her finger. Now her hand trembled, not from the ring, but from the all the tiny electric pulses charging from his touch.

"It fits," she observed, amazed.

"So do we."

Chapter 20

Hotel Principe Di Savoia's five-star Galleria was celebrated for impeccable cuisine. Tonight it was also the stage for Ryan's and Joey's masterful performances as a newly engaged couple.

As Joey glided past the hotel's check-in counter, she recognized the tall, lanky young man who'd cut up her credit card and, judging by his sudden double take, she guessed that he'd recognized her, too. She favored him with a triumphant smile and clung tighter to her escort.

"I see you're already getting the hang of this," Ryan whispered, mistaking her smile.

"Practice makes perfect."

They continued their stroll across the hotel's grand marble flooring until they reached the restaurant's door. The establishment's host, a distinguished septuagenar-

ian with a silver widow's peak, glanced up from his
long reservation list and instantly recognized Ryan.

"Ah, Signore Donovan. We were thrilled to learn
you and your beautiful guest would be dining with us
this evening."

"This beautiful guest is my fiancée," Ryan amended.

The host took the correction with a smile. "My apol-
ogies, *signore*." He looked to Joey and gave a half bow.
"I'm pleased to inform you that your table is ready," he
said. "If you will follow me."

"Ready?" Ryan whispered.

She drew a deep breath, stilled her wobbling legs and
then nodded to start the show.

Together they fell in line behind their host, and the
moment they entered the main dining room, all eyes,
whether blatantly or covertly, followed them.

Joey could hardly breathe let alone smile and gaze
adoringly at the man whose arm she still clutched like
her personal life-support machine. Yet somehow she
managed.

"Who the hell is she?" Carlina hissed as her bejeweled fingers gripped her salad fork. Her eyes narrowed
and then widened as they roamed over each diamond
that clung to the mysterious girl's ears, neck, wrist, and
hand. "She looks familiar."

Laurence would have answered, but he was almost
certain that his eyes were playing tricks on him. It simply
couldn't be. But when the woman's soft laugh drifted
over to him, he knew there was no mistaking it. "Jo-Jo."

"What?" Carlina's head snapped toward him.
"Your Jo-Jo?"

"Well, technically she's not my Jo-Jo anymore." He laughed, but his fiancée looked far from being amused.

"What is she still doing with Ryan...wearing an engagement ring?"

"What?" He half stood out of his chair to see for himself, but Carlina quickly pulled him back down into his chair.

"Don't look so obvious," she snapped. A scowl marred her once-beautiful features and then, as she forcibly composed herself, it disappeared.

Another bubble of Joey's laughter floated throughout the room, and Laurence squirmed in his seat as though he waited for a root canal. It didn't make sense. Joey, honest almost to a fault, had stated that she wasn't dating anyone else. So how was it possible that within a week's time she was sporting a ring from one of Hollywood's powerful directors?

Hollywood moves fast, but this had to be a record.

"Larry, did you hear me?" Carlina hissed at him again.

"No, dear," he said with his gaze still piercing across the room. "What did you say?"

"I *said* I want to know what's going on with them."

"You're not the only one."

Joey opened her mouth and allowed Ryan to plop a piece of their delicious Italian bread into her mouth and then moaned seductively. "That is good."

"You keep moaning like that and I'm going to have to cut your boy when he comes over here to try and steal you away."

She laughed at his confidence. "I seriously doubt that he will come—"

"Ryan," Carlina's syrupy voice interrupted. "What a surprise seeing you here."

Ryan cast a quick glance over his shoulder. "Not really." He returned his attention to Joey. "The American cast is staying at the same hotel. It's reasonable to think we'll bump into each other during mealtime, as well."

Joey smiled and kept her eyes locked on Ryan, mostly because she was afraid to look at Laurence—afraid that he would see through her performance. After all, she'd only been an actress for twenty minutes.

"Aren't you going to say hello, Jo-Jo?"

Damn. Slowly, calmly, she glanced up, widened her eyes to the appropriate degree to convey surprise, and then laughed. "Laurence, I didn't see you standing there."

Ryan squeezed her hand. Had she blown her cover?

Laurence nodded with his eyes searing into hers. "I can't tell you how stunned I am to see you here. One would think you followed me."

"The only person she was following was me," Ryan said, and brought her diamonded hand to his lips. "Isn't that right, sweetheart?"

Joey turned her gaze back to Ryan as she inched closer to him. "You know I would follow you anywhere, honey."

Ryan winked. "So how's that jaw healing up, Dr. Benson? It looks like the swelling has gone down."

"You're lucky I didn't sue—"

"Larry." No one missed the warning in Carlina's voice. "You're talking to *my* director."

An ugly war raged across Laurence's face before he

finally clamped his mouth shut, but when Ryan brushed a butterfly kiss against Joey's nose he spat out a question. "How long have you two been together?"

Ryan answered again. "Long enough for me to know that I want to spend the rest of my life with her."

Though she knew his words were lies, Joey's heart still fluttered, and her face heated with embarrassment at the compliment.

"May I?" Carlina reached for Joey's hand before she had a chance to refuse her inquiry. "Ah, looks like about six carats." She tossed an angry glare at her fiancé.

"You know your diamonds," Ryan complimented.

Their waiter appeared. "Will you two be joining Mr. Donovan's party?"

"Yes," Carlina answered, and then sent her million-dollar smile toward Ryan and Joey. "Dinner is on me. I want to be the first to congratulate the happy couple."

"Well," Ryan pretended to be a little put off. "We were sort of hoping to have a *private* celebration."

"You'll have plenty of time for that later." Laurence joined in on the game and took one of the chairs the staff had added to Ryan's table.

Carlina cleared her throat, and Laurence bounced back up to pull out a chair for her. "Thank you, *dear.*"

Joey shared a bemused grin with her date and then surprised herself by leaning forward to steal a kiss.

Ryan met her lips with an eager tenderness that caused both of them to momentarily forget about their guests.

Laurence cleared his throat.

Joey shied back and apologized. "We tend to get carried away," she offered as an excuse.

"Apparently." Laurence sulked as the waiter poured everyone fresh drinks. "I guess you pulled the wool over my eyes."

She frowned. "What do you mean?"

"Come, now." He straightened in his chair. "I've never seen you like this. The hair, the clothes—you've changed."

Joey suddenly felt like a fraud. "I haven't changed that much. I'm still a woman who wants to plant roots and watch them grow."

"Six roots, if I remember correctly."

"Six?" Carlina chuckled in horror. "Don't you think that's a little too…domestic? Do you know what that many kids could do to a woman's figure?"

"Actually," Ryan said, butting in, "I was hoping for more. Seven—maybe eight?"

"Eight children?" Carlina questioned. "You? Come now, Ryan. You must be pulling my leg."

"Why is that so hard to believe?" he challenged. "How long do you think a man can go through life, filling his house with useless things? Things that can't love you back or give measure to a life. Children are a slice of immortality. Who wouldn't want that?"

Tears glistened in Joey's eyes, and she quickly lowered them before she embarrassed herself.

"Well, I never quite thought about it that way," Laurence admitted, his attention settling back on Joey.

Ryan took things a step farther as he lifted Joey's chin so that their eyes met. "I can hardly wait to have girls with dark, mesmerizing eyes, rich flawless skin and smiles that remind me each time how lucky I am for marrying their mother."

"The boys," Joey whispered, "will grow to be strong

and tall, and no matter how well we teach them, they'll never quite have hearts as big and tender as their father."

A light twinkled in Ryan's eyes, and this time it was he who leaned forward and captured another kiss.

Emotions Joey had never experienced, let alone named, crashed through her and uprooted everything she'd ever known. Suddenly she was confused or caught up in her own web of lies.

Throughout dinner Ryan and Joey continued to have eyes only for each other, and more than a few times she thought Laurence's gaze was going to burn a hole through her head. But before dessert was served, Carlina made an announcement.

"I better visit the little girl's room. Jo, would you care to join me?"

I'd rather go skinny-dipping in a tank full of white sharks. "Sure."

Ryan jumped from his seat and quickly helped Joey from her chair.

"Try not to miss me," she flirted.

"You know I will." He kissed her cheek and watched her walk away.

During the walk to the ladies' room, Joey wondered whether she was going to have to throw punches in her beautiful white gown once they reached their destination. It's not that she wouldn't mind; it's just that she really would hate to get blood all over it.

Carlina pushed through the door and checked around before she waltzed over to the large, rectangular mirror before the sinks.

"I have to hand it to you," Carlina said saucily. "You're one smooth operator. I've never seen Ryan so completely whipped—and so quickly. What's your secret?"

Joey folded her arms. "I don't follow you."

"Oh, we're going to play that game, are we?" Carlina turned toward her. Her eyes glinted like the wicked witch of the west. "You can't outslick a can of oil, dear. I know a gold digger when I see one. And you're the best one I've seen in a long time. Eight children—please!"

"I'm confused," Joey admitted. "You're engaged but yet you're acting like you're jealous of me and Ryan."

"I'm jealous of no woman," Carlina seethed. "I can get any man, anytime. I took Laurence, didn't I? And right from under your nose."

"That's one way of looking at it." Joey stepped toward the woman and met her gaze daringly. "Or you can say I took Ryan right from under yours. If you ask me, I got the better deal."

Chapter 21

"What a bitch!" Joey seethed as she stormed through the suite door behind her fiancé. "I can't believe Larry dumped me for her."

"Laurence," Ryan corrected.

"Bite me," she snapped, and pulled the pins from her hair. "Do you know she actually had the gall to call me a gold digger?"

"Well, to be fair—our engagement is sort of out of the blue. People may think that."

"Do *you* think that?"

"Of course not." He drew her into his arms and smiled when her body surrendered against him. "I told you before, I think you're perfect."

She shook her head and pulled away. "You can stop that now. We're alone."

"Stop what?"

Joey looked at him. "Stop looking at me as though you're making love to me. Stop saying everything I've always wanted to hear. Love. Children. Immortality. It's starting to turn out that the best relationship I ever had never happened." She glanced down and stared at her hand through a thin sheen of tears. "Look at this ring. A week ago I would have killed for a ring like this. I still might. Is it really six carats?"

"Something like that." Ryan smiled. "You know, uh, Carlina suggested we go over a few things in her script…around one in the morning—about an hour from now. Did, uh, Larry make his move?"

Joey dropped her hands. "He slipped me a note."

"And?"

She shrugged. "He wants me to try to get away so we can talk about…returning a few items we still have at each other's places."

"He has clothes hanging in your closet?"

Another shrug. "A few."

Ryan nodded and slid his hands into his pants pockets. "Are you going to go?"

"It's sort of silly not to." She shifted and twisted the ring on her finger. "What about you? Are you going to go discuss *scripts* with the dragon lady?"

"I did promise you I would help—"

"Yeah, but I don't want it to seem like I'm sort of pimping you out or anything."

"No, I'll be happy to do it," he protested, but felt like a dunce when her face collapsed.

"Oh." Joey shuffled past him. "Then I better go get changed."

"Yeah." He nodded. "Me, too."

* * *

It was a little more difficult for Laurence and Carlina to sneak off to their separate, secret rendezvous—but it wasn't impossible. They returned to their suite—all smiles, fake sunshine and hidden agendas.

Laurence decided to fake an emergency medical call from his practice. Given the time difference, he was fairly certain Carlina would fall for it. Other than free nips and tucks, she rarely asked questions about his practice.

Keep your lies short, sweet, and she will never suspect a thing, he assured himself. At least, he hoped.

"Well, dinner was highly amusing." Carlina broke their silence as she sat on the bed and removed her pumps.

"Oh, how so?" He played dumb. However, judging by the sharp edge of her stare, it wasn't such a good idea. "Oh, you mean Jo-Jo and Donovan?"

"What else would I mean?" she sulked. "Seems your ex wasted no time getting over you."

"What is that supposed to mean?" His defenses snapped to attention.

"Nothing, darling." Her voice oozed honey, but her smile remained as tight as a patient's first face lift. "I just mean I was stunned."

So was he. "Did either of them mention when the happy occasion would be?"

"They really didn't talk much, since they were too busy cramming their tongues down each other's throats." She shuddered. "It was disgusting."

The vision of Joey when she first floated into the restaurant with a swirl of bubbly laughter replayed in his mind. "Yeah…disgusting." He turned away from Carlina.

Laurence had always known that Joey was attractive,

but more in a cutesy way. He had no idea she could transform into such a polished gem.

"And that nonsense about eight children," Carlina harped, slithering out of her black dress. "Did you buy all of that?"

"Jo-Jo always wanted a big family. She's the fourth of six children. I believe one of her sisters has five children. It was nothing we saw eye-to-eye on, but…"

Caution seeped into Carlina's voice. "But what?"

He shrugged. "That speech Donovan made about immortality—"

"What about it?"'

"I don't know. It has a certain ring of truth to it, don't you think?"

Carlina's face collapsed while her eyes bulged with horror.

"Plus, babies are the new fashion accessory in Hollywood," he quickly added.

Just as quickly Carlina's expression turned thoughtful. "That *is* true."

Laurence nodded, but there was something else that Ryan said that really had him thinking. *I can hardly wait to have girls with dark, mesmerizing eyes, rich flawless skin, and smiles that remind me each time how lucky I am for marrying their mother.*

If ever there was a woman who could produce beautiful babies, it would his Jo-Jo. *His.* Laurence turned the word over in his mind. How was it that another man had replaced him in her heart so fast? Last week she was in love with him.

Sure, Joey could be a little fickle from time to time, but her feelings for him were real—weren't they?

Laurence snatched off his tie and slid out of his suit jacket. Later tonight he would get his answers, and he was more than confident he could prove that Joey Adams was still in love with him.

Joey selected a simple black dress with a pink cardigan sweater from her new wardrobe. A part of her wanted to dress to impress; the other part didn't want to come off looking as if she was trying too hard. She removed all her jewelry except for the eye-popping engagement ring.

When she stepped out of her bedroom, she hadn't expected to bump into Ryan, still dressed in this evening's dinner suit.

"Ah, nice choice," he complimented, handing her a flute of champagne. "I figured you'd need this before you raced out of here."

She accepted the drink with trembling hands. "Thanks."

He smiled, but his eyes were hard with disappointment. "Have you prepared what you're going to say to him tonight?"

"Prepared?"

"When he starts interrogating you about us." Ryan walked in a circle around her. Occasionally he brushed his body against her. "First thing he'd want to know is if you're truly in love with me. Then he'd want to know *when* you fell in love with me, and then lastly—do you still love him?"

"Oh." Joey's body stiffened each time he touched her. "Well then, I guess I'll tell him that I love you more than life itself."

Ryan stopped walking. "What is it that you love about me?"

She glanced up at him. "What?"

"In case he asks."

"I, uh, I love how when I do something silly—like getting wedged in a men's bathroom window—you're there when I fall."

"Land is more like it." He chuckled and lightened the mood.

She smiled and continued, "I love how you've become like a knight in shining armor—showing up every time I need rescuing."

"A knight, huh?" He shook his head. "Might want to keep that under wraps. It could ruin my reputation."

"Don't get me wrong. You still have asshole tendencies."

They laughed and sipped their drinks. The thought that she should be leaving to meet Laurence crossed her mind, but she made no move toward the door. Instead, she drained her glass in one long gulp.

"How about another one?" he asked, but there was a hidden meaning in his eyes. *Stay with me tonight.*

Joey's pulse leaped and her knees trembled as she realized one thing: she was exactly where she wanted to be. "I'd love another drink."

Laurence was spared having to tell Carlina his grand lie when she emerged from the bathroom dressed in a sleek black-and-white pantsuit and stating she and her assistant had arranged to read lines before her first day of shooting.

If he weren't so eager to see Jo-Jo again, he would've

questioned such a strange arrangement at a strange hour. As it was, he bade his fiancée good-night and made a show of yawning and stretching before heading off to bed.

However, the moment the door shut behind Carlina, he peeled the sheet off and climbed out of bed. He'd asked Jo-Jo to meet him in the gardens around one. If he hurried, he would just make it.

He dressed in a flash and charged out of his suite like a man on mission. As he rushed down the hall, he couldn't believe how hard and fast his heart pounded at the thought of seeing his Jo-Jo.

She didn't love Donovan; she couldn't. At most he was a rebound guy. All he needed was a few minutes alone with her, and once again she would be wrapped around his finger. Maybe he should see about getting a separate suite. He could prove to her how much he still cared for her.

But what about Carlina?

Laurence quickly shook that troubling question from his head. Determined, he would cross that bridge when he came to it. Right now he wanted Jo-Jo to confess she still had feelings for him.

Heck, if she just showed up, he would have his answer. A few minutes later he strolled out of his hotel and into its beautiful but cold gardens where he waited and waited…and waited.

Chapter 22

Joey didn't leave after her second drink or after her third. In fact, while the night flowed effortlessly into another day, she and Ryan stood out on the breezy terrace, soaking in the panoramic view of Milan.

They stood close to each other, but not close enough, not as close as they would like. Each behaved as though waiting for the right sign or body language to move in close.

"It's so beautiful here." She sighed. "I can see why so many people love it."

Ryan followed her gaze and nodded in lazy appreciation as he puffed on his cigar. "I've been here four days and I hadn't taken the time to stop and notice."

"And now that you have?" she asked, glancing over at him.

"Now that I have, I know it's just one more thing that's not as beautiful as you."

The warmth of his words sustained her, despite the freezing temperature. "You're working awfully hard to win your bet."

"Of course I am." Ryan finally inched closer. "Look what I'll win." He stood straight as an arrow and stared at her full lips. Lord, how he wanted her—and not just for the night. That realization stunned him. "How long does it take for a person to fall in love?" he asked suddenly.

Joey blinked. "I…I don't know."

His eyes deserted her lips to travel back up to her eyes. "No?"

She shrugged, thinking. "My oldest sister, Sheldon, said she fell in love with husband, Edwin, the moment she laid eyes on him at a roller-skating rink."

"Love at first sight?" He erased another inch.

"She swears by it."

"And how about you? Are you a believer?"

"I'm starting to think that I don't know what I believe anymore," she answered truthfully.

The white puffs of air from their chilled breathing blended together.

"Do you think he's still waiting for you?" he asked.

"Who?"

He smiled.

"Oh, uh, I don't know." She frowned, wondering where her head was.

"Do you care?"

Joey's heart leaped into her throat while she battled whether to tell the truth. However, Ryan didn't wait for her to answer, instead he finally erased the last few inches between them, tossed his cigar over the terrace and drew Joey into his arms.

She loved the taste of him. He was a unique blend of brandy, spearmint and Cuban cigars. The latter gave him the taste of danger and raw masculinity.

The very thing she'd come to love about him.

Ryan's large hands gently made quick work of her sweater's small buttons. When he slid it off her body, she shivered against him.

"Shouldn't we go back inside?" she asked.

"I'll go wherever you want to go," he said breathlessly, now attacking the buttons on the back of her dress.

Joey gently stilled his hand, and when his probing gaze lifted, she smiled. "Then take me to the bedroom."

"I'm feeling a strange sense of déjà vu," he admitted.

Her lips grew even wider. "Trust me. Sleep is the last thing on my mind."

Grinning, Ryan swept her into his arms. "Does this mean I'm finally going to get laid?"

She pulled his face close and branded him with a kiss. "Yes, Mr. Donovan. That's exactly what it means."

"Hallelujah!" He twirled her in a wide circle, and she giggled as though breathless from a roller-coaster ride. Within seconds he crossed the spacious presidential suite and kicked open the door of the bedroom Joey had slept in the previous night.

All the while Joey convinced herself that she was out of her mind. What she was doing defied all reason—and yet she couldn't stop herself. Nor could she explain the cluster of butterflies that raced through every inch of her body.

One thing was certain: she had never felt this way with…what was his name?

He placed her onto the bed and sat down next to her. For a long moment the couple was satisfied to just gaze upon each other as if they were burning the other's features into their memory. Ryan liked every angle of her face, loved the plumpness of her lips and was completely crazy about her eyes. Perfect.

Joey couldn't decide on what she loved more: the way his long lashes framed his dark eyes or the slight crookedness of his nose. She sighed. What the hell was happening to her?

Ryan reached for the top button of her dress, and again she stopped him.

Joey smiled. "I want to do you first."

His lips curled. "Then by all means."

Slowly she sat up and reached for the clear buttons of his starched shirt. Her fingers trembled, but they worked steadily. Moments later she flung it and his T-shirt to the floor.

Taking her time, Joey rubbed the contours of his solid, wide chest. Then, as if mesmerized, she leaned closer and ran her tongue along the same trail. Soon her mouth found its way to his shoulder, his neck and at long last settled to nibble on his earlobe.

Ryan's long, lean fingers resumed their work on her dress, and in no time the thin material joined his clothes on the floor.

One look at the black-and-red lacy lingerie and Ryan made a mental note to send Sergio an extra tip and add him to next year's Christmas list. After that, his thoughts muddled. Joey's hand fumbled at his pants buckle while her hot mouth still suckled his ear.

He was too anxious, too excited. If he didn't cool things off a bit, things might be coming to a head prematurely.

"Not yet, baby." He pulled her hand away and leaned her back onto the bed.

Joey sighed as he stretched out above her while his hand stroked her inner thighs. He smiled, nuzzled his face in her chest and tugged open the small bow nestled there with his teeth. In no time at all, he greedily filled his mouth with one and then the other breast, his tongue glazing each bud to a polished finish. Then finally he bit at them, pulled them this way and then that as if to get a feel of their full weight.

The painful pulse in his pants became a merciless throb; he fought all that was holy to maintain his current pace. His hands soon deserted her thighs to roam across the flat plains of her belly and then slipped beneath the borders of her panties to graze over a vee of downy soft curls.

Another sigh tumbled from her lips the moment his fingers entered her slick passage. Her hips immediately lifted from the bed in a polite homecoming.

"You like that, baby?"

Joey tried to talk, but her head was too dizzy, her body too hot.

"I didn't hear you, baby." Ryan's baritone turned husky with passion. "I want you to tell me."

"Y-yes! Oh please, don't stop."

"But I've got something better for you." As quick as a whip, he wrenched the panties down her hips and legs and flung them to join the other clothing. He pushed up and ravished her mouth with a kiss that curled her toes and stirred her soul.

Before her arms could enfold him, he vanished. But his mouth and his tongue were placed on another pair of lips.

Joey squirmed to the head of the bed, but Ryan's strong arms locked around her thighs and dragged her back toward him and his invading tongue.

Breathing seemed impossible, and soon a galaxy of stars danced before Joey's eyes, while heat scorched her from all sides. If she could just get away, she might be able to save herself.

But Ryan's hold was firm, his mouth and tongue relentless.

Joey bit her lower lip and managed to draw in short pants of air. Tiny ripples of something glorious threaded through her body; her hands drifted down to hold his head in place; her legs wrapped and squeezed him tight.

Her sighs became moans and then finally cries of ecstasy when her first orgasm rocked her world. However, Ryan's mouth persisted, and her bid for freedom or a reprieve renewed her efforts to escape.

"Please, please. I can't breathe," she begged.

Ryan chuckled and released his hold. "Well, we can't have that now. Can we?" He climbed off the bed and removed the last of his clothes.

At first sight of Ryan's…equipment, Joey blinked and then blinked again. How was she gonna…? Could she handle…?

"Don't worry," he said, unwrapping a Magnum wrapper. "I'll be gentle."

"Wait." A nervous excitement coursed through Joey. "May I?"

Ryan's smile widened as he handed over the condom. "By all means." He stepped closer to the bed with no worries about whether he would be able to maintain his erection. In fact, the moment Joey's hand slid around his thick shaft, he knew nothing was going to disturb this groove.

However, Joey's assistance quickly turned into torture. Her long fingers were as smooth as silk and her light handling had him struggling for control. Yet one look at her face and it was clear that she knew exactly what she was doing.

"Payback is a bitch." She winked.

"It's not over." He eased her away and finished sliding the condom on before stretching out, once again, above her. He started his playful loitering with her breasts again and purposely allowed the weight of his arousal to press against her inner thigh.

In no time at all, she panted his name and begged him to enter her. He relished the sound of her soft pleas, but only toyed with her when he placed just the tip inside and then feasted his hand and mouth on different areas.

"Please, please." Joey tried to ease him inside, but he refused to relinquish his control.

"Do you think you can handle it?" he whispered.

She didn't know, but she was more than willing to give it a try.

"I didn't hear you."

"Yes, Yes. Please."

True to his word, Ryan was more than gentle when entered her. A fine sheen of perspiration beaded his forehead as her body sheathed him in a way like no other. After a few breathing exercises, he was content to wait until she adjusted to his size, but she was the first one to move—slowly but surely.

He allowed her to set the pace, a smooth, hypnotic rhythm that made his eyes loll inside his head. He stopped a few times to make sure that he wasn't hurting her, but by the third time, she swore she'd kill him if he stopped again.

No thought penetrated Joey's purple haze, she just allowed herself to enjoy every feeling Ryan's lovemaking brought to life. Everything he did felt new and exciting.

He frequently picked it up, flipped it, and rubbed her down to the point where the sheets pasted themselves to their bodies.

One, two, three orgasms shot through her and slammed her down and still her body begged for more. Either the second or the third condom popped, but the forth and fifth held strong.

Sometime before 5:00 a.m., the lovers fell into a deep slumber, but Ryan's internal clock woke him at 6:00 a.m. and reminded him he had a film to direct.

"Where are you going?" Joey asked with one eye at half-mast and the other closed.

"I have to go to work." He pried himself from the long chaise and wondered briefly how they'd moved so far from the bed.

"You have to go now?" She forced herself to stand, and then lazily looped her arms around his neck.

They'd both been sexed up and spit out, but one look at her beautiful naked body and Ryan's soldier was ready for another salute.

Joey glanced down. "You can't go to work like that."
She took him by the hand and led him back to the bed.
"Well, maybe just for a few more minutes…"

Chapter 23

By the time Franklin Adams Casey sat down to dinner, it was ice-cold…and she was still alone. Another day meant another excuse why George couldn't make it home for dinner. *Why am I surprised?* she thought.

She tossed down her fork. A migraine exploded when it clanged against her good china. Fifteen years of marriage, and more nights than she cared to admit she slept alone.

She wasn't so sure she could say the same thing for her husband.

Thoughts of hiring a private detective flitted in and out of her mind, but what would she do if her worst fears were true? Would she divorce George—give up the life to which she'd become accustomed?

Worst of all, could she go back to being single? She

was already staring down the barrel of forty, and just seeing what Peyton and Michael went through and what Joey was still going through was enough to give her nightmares.

Maybe it was okay to be married in name only. Maybe she should just hang on a little longer. Maybe.

"So what do you think is going on with Michael?" Peyton asked Sheldon as she bounced one of her nieces on her hip.

"There's no telling with Mike. She may always be quick to jump into our business, but she's always been pretty tight-lipped when it comes to sharing details about her own life."

"You think something's going on with her and Phillip?"

"I'd be surprised if there wasn't." Sheldon pulled the last baby from the tub and bundled her up in a bath towel. "I mean, look how long it took to get him to the altar."

"But they've only been married, like, a year and a half."

"And she's been acting funny for the last six months." Sheldon led Peyton to one of the children's room and continued to get the children ready for bed. "I don't suggest we press her, though. She'll tell us when she's ready."

Peyton nodded, but she remained troubled. It was odd to think of Michael not in control of something. From her job at the bank to organizing family reunions, Michael was the glue that kept the family together.

On one hand, it just didn't seem right to wait until the glue eroded before they offered to help. However, she suspected Sheldon was right. Michael was pretty bullheaded and wouldn't want her sisters wiggling their noses in her affairs. It was hypocrisy with a capital *H*, but what could you do?

Minutes later she and Sheldon kissed the children good-night and went downstairs to collapse on the sofa.

"I don't see how you do it," Peyton huffed. A day with Sheldon and the kids left her more exhausted than the eighty hours she put into her art agency.

"It's hard at first but once you get yourself on a schedule, it's smooth sailing." She laughed. "And if you buy that I have some swampland out in Florida I want to sell you."

Peyton laughed and squinted at the television. She recognized the show *Entertainment Tonight,* but was stunned by the picture the show flashed. "Hey, isn't that Joey's ex?"

Sheldon followed her gaze and picked up the remote. "I think you're right."

"Sources say there may be trouble in paradise for actress Carlina Leoni and her new fiancé, Dr. Laurence Benson. Witnesses have spotted the couple arguing around the set of Carlina's latest picture, *La Bella Vida.*"

"You don't think Joey has anything to do with this?" Sheldon asked.

"I'd be surprised if she didn't."

"While one engagement maybe in trouble on the Italian set another one is brewing. Sources are saying the once confirmed bachelor and director Ryan Donovan may also be tying the knot with this mystery woman…

A picture of Joey, splendid in a floor-length white

gown, flashed onto the screen, and both Sheldon and Peyton screamed in recognition.

"Oh, my God!" Sheldon gasped.

"Shhh. I want to hear the rest of this," Peyton said.

"We may not know the name of Donovan's new lady love, but a person would have to be blind to miss the rock on her finger."

At the end of the report, the two sisters turned to each other with wide eyes and open mouths. Before either of them could put voice to their stunned thoughts, Sheldon's phone rang.

"Michael," they said in unison and they raced over to the phone.

Sheldon placed the call on speaker phone.

"You won't believe what I just saw on *ET* tonight."

"We saw it," Peyton and Sheldon answered.

"I knew we should have gone to Italy," Michael huffed. "Joey has gone off and done something stupid!"

"Now, now. We don't know that," Sheldon said, trying to calm her down.

"They're saying she's engaged—to a man she couldn't have known more than five days."

"They could be wrong," Peyton reasoned.

"Did you not see all those diamonds around her neck and her ears…and Mary Hartman said something about a big rock on her finger." Michael continued to be agitated. "I hate being left out in the dark."

"Well, look on the bright side," Peyton said, shrugging. "At least she's not coming back home with that jerk Laurence."

A silence buzzed over the line for a few seconds.

"You know, P.J.," Michael said. "When you're right, you're right. I just wish we knew what the hell is going on."

Carlina Leoni was pissed. In the two days since Ryan started showing off his fiancée, all anyone talked about was the size of the ring he'd placed on the woman's finger. Another bee in her bouquet was the fact Ryan had unapologetically stood her up the other night. And to add insult to injury, he now allowed the hussy to hang around the set.

"I want a new ring," Carlina snapped at Laurence through her cell phone as she stormed into her set trailer. "Everybody is making a big deal about that big nobody's engagement ring. No one is saying anything about mine." She huffed and paced back in forth. "I know we've been over this. We're going over it again. I want a new ring or the wedding is off." She snapped her phone closed, pitched it to the other end of the small trailer, just missing her assistant's head by a few inches.

Laurence slammed the phone down while his blood pressure threatened to explode. His once sweet, submissive fiancée had turned into a self-absorbed egomaniac. "Buy her another ring," he mumbled under his breath. "She must have fallen and bumped her head."

For the past two days, he and Carlina did nothing but argue. And when their arguments reached the tabloids, they sulked more and more inside their suite. When Carlina announced this morning she wanted to postpone their nuptials until they returned stateside, Laurence knew his engagement was on the rocks.

He paced their suite like a caged lion while his perfect plans for his perfect future crashed against the sharp edges of reality. More and more, he realized he had proposed to the wrong woman. It didn't help that every time he turned around, whether it was shopping through Centro Bonola, or wandering through Musei del Castello, Ryan and Joey were already there.

Each time he ran into Joey, everything about her glowed. And that bastard Donovan acted as though he couldn't keep his hands off her. Actually, it was pretty sickening to watch their public display of affection. It wasn't like they didn't have a room where they could carry out that sort of thing.

Though Laurence stopped pacing, his mind still raced with thoughts and memories of Joey. Though she was a low rung on the Hollywood ladder, she never allowed herself to get caught up in the rat race. Family was the most important thing to her; she never made any bones about it. The reason he easily dated other women was because Joey never once tried to suffocate him or install a Lojack on his pager.

She trusted him—and then he betrayed that trust.

"Stupid, stupid, stupid." There had to be something he could do—some way he could win her back. Yet how could he compete with the likes of a big mover and shaker like Donovan?

"There has to be some way."

"I have to hand it to you," Zach thundered, slapping Ryan across the back. "When you set out to win, you go balls out."

The two friends met during a brief break near the set's catered buffet.

"Keep your voice down," Ryan hissed, glancing around and tugging him aside. "Someone might hear you."

"Engaged." Zach chuckled. "I predicted it, but I preferred a *real* engagement over a fake one."

Carlina was strolling toward the buffet for a bowl of fruit and an iced bottle of water when Zach Griffin's words halted her.

"What do you mean you didn't know the news would hit the papers?" Zach whispered conspiratorially.

Carlina ducked behind a set prop and leaned in closer.

"I'm a director, not a headline-hungry actor where every move I make is scrutinized by America's desperate housewives."

"Then you shouldn't have bought such a stunning ring."

"*You* bought the ring."

Zach shrugged. "I can't help I have good taste."

"Very funny." Ryan thought about it and withdrew a cigar. "It is a nice ring."

"See? Don't I always look out for you?"

"Let's not get delusional."

Carlina's eyes grew wide as silver dollars. *A fake engagement?* She was suddenly giddy as a schoolgirl. Ryan Donovan had pulled a classic Hollywood stunt. It all made sense.

She turned around and sprinted back to her trailer. All was not lost.

Zach chuckled. "I hear you, I hear you. I'm still

working on your financing. I should hear something in the next few days."

"Famous last words."

"But tell me something, man." Zach's voice lowered. "How long are you going to keep this pretense up? You got what you wanted out of the deal, right? It's cost you a pretty penny so you had to have hit it by now."

"Don't talk like that about Joey."

Zach frowned. "I'm confused. This was an act, right?"

Ryan's gaze dropped, his words lodged in his throat.

"Oh my God. You've really fallen for her, haven't you?"

"So what if I have?" he asked defensively. "It's not the end of the world." He straightened his shoulders. "Besides, wasn't it you who said it was time that I settled down?"

"Oh my God."

"Stop saying that," Ryan snapped.

"I don't know what else to say," Zach stammered. He looked like he needed to sit down. "You always said that you didn't believe in holy matrimony."

Ryan shrugged. "A man can change his mind."

"The phrase is 'a woman can change her mind.' Men just surrender."

"Fine." A grin spread wide across his face. "I happily surrender."

Chapter 24

Joey escaped back to Ryan's suite to get a jump on preparing for another glorious evening out. She didn't know where they were going, but she was certain they would have a great time. They always had fun.

Last night they did nothing more than race nude in the suite's private swimming pool. Ryan might have more muscles, but she was a natural fish in the water. Of course, the highlight of the night was making love in the pool, the Jacuzzi, and the Turkish bath. They'd also made out in each of the three bedrooms, the formal dining room, on top of the piano and at last on the terrace. In a roundabout way, she finally had the full tour of the place.

"Impotent, my ass." She laughed and wrapped on a robe. Smiling and humming, she crossed the room to head toward her closet but stopped by the phone. She really should call home, yet just the thought of Mike's tongue-lashing made her shy away.

However, she had to call before the whole brigade rammed down her door, knocked her out and dragged her bloody body back home. She chuckled under her breath, and then stopped when she realized that the scenario had possibilities.

Joey picked up the phone and decided the safest sister to call was Peyton. Unfortunately, Peyton was bound by certain obligations and after first checking to see if she was all right, switched to a second line to call Frankie who called Sheldon who at last called Michael.

"Whoa. Whoa. Calm down. Calm down," she said, to no avail. The line hummed with threats and notes of concern.

"I ought to kill you," Michael started in.

"We were worried about you," Sheldon chastised.

"Joey, we did call the police," Frankie added.

"I'm fine. I'm fine," Joey assured. "I know I shouldn't have run off like that, but…I needed to handle something on my own."

"And how does that include getting involved with a big-time movie producer?" Sheldon asked.

"Director," Frankie corrected.

"And the word is *engaged*," Michael also corrected. "You want to explain that?"

"How did you hear about—"

"Are you kidding? It was on *Entertainment Tonight*," Michael snapped.

"I just saw it on the cover of one of the tabloids at the grocery store," Sheldon informed them. "Is your ring as big as they say?"

"Six carats," Joey said, and held up her hand to admire the beautiful gem. "You should see it." Realizing what she said, Joey's smile eroded. The diamond was given to her as part of a charade.

The girls whistled, impressed.

"Frankie, it sounds like she has you beat by three carats," Peyton teased.

"I ain't mad at her." Frankie laughed. "Welcome to the big diamond club."

"Hey!" the other girls intoned.

"Everyone knows that it's not the size that counts," Sheldon said.

"That little diamond dust Edwin gave you back in high school barely qualifies as a ring," Frankie joked.

"Hear, hear," Michael, Peyton and Joey agreed.

"Whatever," Sheldon laughed. "If you ask me, if a man gives you a big diamond it's to compensate for what he's lacking in other areas, if you know what I mean."

"I can personally testify that's a huge lie," Joey said.

A round of girlish giggles and moans of "Oh, my" filtered over the line, and soon after they all clamored for "Details, details."

"I don't kiss and tell," Joey said.

"Since when?" the sisters demanded in unison.

They were right. Joey knew how to gossip with the best of them. She hedged a bit longer and then finally spilled the beans about Ryan's…equipment.

"Oh, my." Sheldon sounded faint.

"You're lying," Michael and Frankie accused.

"Have you seen a doctor?" Peyton asked.

Joey laughed at their reaction, but also decided to come clean about the something else.

"What do you mean that you're not really engaged?" Michael shouted. "What the hell have you gotten yourself into?"

"Nothing. Ryan was just trying to help me win Larry—I mean, Laurence back. It started out all pretty innocent. I don't think he thought any of this would reach the tabloids."

"He bought you a six carat ring…for a pretend engagement?" Michael asked. "What kind of nut job would do something like that?"

"I think it's kind of sweet," Sheldon said dreamily.

"You would," Michael and Frankie accused.

"Did it work?" Peyton asked.

"Did what work?" Joey asked confused.

"Did Laurence fall for it?"

"Hook, line and sinker," Joey admitted. Her shoulders drooped with growing depression.

"So you're the reason Carlina and Laurence have been sighted arguing over there?"

"They have? But how would you—"

"Entertainment Tonight," the sisters answered in sync.

Joey rolled her eyes. "I didn't realize so many eyes were paying attention to us."

"Forget that," Peyton chimed in. "If your plan worked, why are you still wearing this guy's ring? Why aren't you and Laurence on a plane heading back to L.A.?"

"And why are you *sleeping* with your fake fiancé?"

Joey had known the questions were coming, but she'd failed to come up with real answers. How did she explain that she no longer loved Laurence, without sounding flighty or fickle—especially when she had a reputation for being both?

"Joseph?" Peyton asked.

"I'm still here."

"Do you have an answer?"

"Things didn't quite go as planned."

"Meaning you're whipped." Michael read in between the lines.

"I'm not whipped," she protested. "I just decided Larry wasn't what I wanted and there wasn't any reason why I couldn't have a little fun."

"She's whipped," the sisters spoke again in unison.

"Joey, sweetie." Peyton trod lightly. "You're obviously in a very emotional state right now. Why don't you just come home before you end up getting hurt again."

"I'm not going to get hurt. I know what I'm doing."

"Yes. You're lying," Sheldon added. "Not just to the world, but more importantly, to yourself. Nothing good is going to come out of *playing* house."

"Here we go." Joey jumped up. "Mrs. Barefoot and Pregnant is going to give a lecture. Why don't you give it to Michael? She's the one who's pretending and acting like the family doesn't have the good sense God gave us to know she's miserable. Or how about Frankie? She thinks she's pulling the wool over everyone's eyes by showing off what George buys her when we all know he never comes home. Hell, when was the last time any of us has seen George—two Christmases ago?"

Joey paced while her anger boiled over. "If you ask me the only one in a seminormal marriage is Peyton, and I would just as well like to be spared a lecture from her, too."

When she was finished, the line roared with a tense

silence. There was a single click, signifying one of her sisters had hung up.

Joey's heart leaped, and tears of regret burned her eyes. "Oh, God. I'm sorry." She slumped down onto the bed.

"Well," Michael began. "It looks like someone developed a backbone in Italy."

"Yeah," Sheldon croaked. "You must really care for this director guy."

"Peyton, Frankie, are you guys still there?" Joey asked.

"I'm still here," Peyton said. "I guess that means Frankie hung up."

"Damn." Joey sighed. "I really put my foot in my mouth."

"That's putting it lightly," Michael said. "But you had a point…and if you must know, Phillip and I have been separated for the past six months. I think—I think we're going to get a divorce."

"Mike, what happened?" Sheldon asked first.

"Nothing. We should have never gotten married. Looking back on it, I think we did it to save the relationship. It didn't work."

The girls did the best they could to console her over the phone. There were a few sniffles and a whole lot of tears. All the while Joey felt two inches high, and no amount of apologizing made her feel any better.

"Girls, I need to call Frankie back."

"She's not going to answer the phone," Peyton warned. "I'll drive over there and see about her."

"I'll come with," Sheldon chimed.

"I wish I was down there with you guys," Michael said, since she still resided in Los Angeles.

"Me, too," Joey said in earnest. "Since I'm the one who upset her."

"So when *are* you going to end this charade and come back home?" Peyton asked, her voice still laden with concern.

It was a good question, Joey realized, and one that deserved an answer. "I'll need a ticket."

"I'll call the airport right now," Peyton promised.

Joey nodded and hung up the phone. Fat teardrops leaked from her eyes as she stared down at the diamond on her finger. Her sisters were right, only pain would come from pretending.

And Ryan knew he'd won his bet the night she didn't meet with Laurence. In fact, they had hardly mentioned his name since then.

She chuckled. Ten days. She had known Ryan only ten days and he had changed her life completely. But was it love or sex on the rebound? One thing was for sure, if she stayed, she'd never find out.

It was time to go home. With her heart wedged in her throat, Joey pulled off her diamond ring and placed it on Ryan's pillow.

Chapter 25

"And cut! That's a wrap," Ryan roared, and stood from his chair. He glanced at his watch and winced at how late taping had gone over. Hopefully a little kissing, a little hugging, and some hot sex would be a sufficient apology for missing dinner.

The crew gave each other a round of applause, and a smiling Carlina sauntered off set. Nothing unusual about it, but there was definitely something to the way she looked at Ryan that puzzled him.

No matter. He shook it off and went over a few more details with the stage crew and his assistant. Another hour and Ryan was the last to leave the set—or so he thought.

"Have a minute?"

Ryan turned toward the angelic voice, though he

was certain whom it belonged to. "Carlina." He glanced around. "What are you still doing here?"

"Waiting to talk to you." Her Cheshire Cat smile grew wider. "Lately, it's almost impossible to get you alone."

He nodded and took a calm step back. "Well, you know how it is, being engaged and all."

She laughed. "Yes, I find it all a little tedious. But one does what one must do for the right press. Right?"

Carlina had his full attention. "What are you talking about?"

She didn't walk so much as slink toward him. "You're a smart man, Ryan. What do you think I'm talking about?"

He lifted his chin as his eyes narrowed.

"Ah. Cat got your tongue?" She continued slinking. "You know, I should have guessed something was up. Some things were a bit *too* coincidental. You and Joey at The Blue Diamond, you punching Laurence, and then both of you showing up here." She stopped just inches before him. "You feel it, too. Don't you?"

Ryan was following along fine until she hit that road bump. "Feel what?"

She leaned up so when she spoke her mint-flavored breath blew against his face. "Feel the electricity flowing between us." Her arms snaked around his neck while her famous curvaceous body pressed against him. "We started something once. What do you say we finish it tonight?"

Ryan laughed. He couldn't help it. It was just that funny. "I don't think that's a good idea." He tried to peel her arms off, but they were like a boa constrictor, the harder he pulled the more they tightened.

"You're going to deny that you punched Larry because you were jealous or that you staged your 'fake engagement' to that skinny nobody just to get my attention?"

Speechless, Ryan stared.

She laughed. "It's okay. I heard you and Mr. Griffin talking earlier. I'm not mad. I'm flattered. And to tell you the truth—I was doing the same thing." She giggled.

"Come again?"

"I accepted Larry's proposal in hopes to make *you* jealous. And it worked!" She launched forward and kissed him soundly on the lips.

A light flashed and Ryan jumped back. "What the hell was that?"

"If you don't know then your fiancée hasn't been doing a good job."

She launched herself at him again, but Ryan's hand shot up before his face and Carlina's lips smacked the center of his palm. "Carlina, stop. You're making a fool of yourself."

She unplanted her lips and he lowered his hand. "You have the wrong idea. I didn't hit Laurence because I was jealous, I hit him because of the way he treated Joey."

"Joey?"

"Yeah. My fake fiancée." He successfully pried her arms off and stepped back. "Only, the pretense is going to turn into reality. I love her—probably from the first time I saw her crawl through the men's bathroom window."

"What?"

He laughed and shook his head. "Nothing. It's a story only our children will hear about."

Carlina looked as though she had a hard time digesting his words. "Then why—"

"I was supposed to be helping her win back her ex-almost-fiancé. But between you, me and the light post, my heart wasn't in it."

"Her what? That doesn't even make sense."

"Try and tell her that." He chuckled.

Carlina remained thunderstruck. "Why on earth would she want Larry back? I just sent him packing." She flashed him her bare left hand.

"She wanted—past tense." His chest swelled. "I'm applying for the position of fiancé—for real this time." Ryan had spent his last two projects trying to capture on film the array of emotions that rippled across Carlina's darkening face. "I'm sorry," he added.

She stared, and then suddenly Carlina burst out laughing. "You almost had me again." She invaded his personal space again. "You and Joey. You and *eight* children—please."

Ryan's face twisted. "What's so funny about that?"

"Come on." Her arms slithered around his neck while her silicon breasts pressed hard into his chest. "Since when were you interested in another man's leftovers?"

He chuckled. "And what does that make you?"

"I was with you first. Remember?" She winked and steered one hand south where it quickly slipped below his pants' waistband.

"Whoa!" Ryan jumped and jerked her arm back up before she had the chance to seize the family jewels. "Chill out. Chill out." He successfully pushed her away.

Carlina's expression crumbled at his body's lack of response. "What the hell is wrong with you? This is the second time I've practically thrown myself at you—"

"Practically?"

"What are you, gay?" She grew taller as her indignity heightened. "Men would kill to be with me!"

"That's it." Ryan latched onto the excuse—anything to get the woman off him. "I'm gay."

"Please." Carlina's eyes nearly rolled to the back of her head. "You're not gay. I know gay when I see gay."

Damn. What does it take to get rid of this woman?

"It's that damn Jo-Jo or Joey. Whatever the hell her damn name is," Carlina snarled. Her rage distorted her beauty. "What is it about that bitch that has you and Larry salivating at her feet?"

"This conversation is over." Ryan turned away from her. "And if you want to stay aboard this production set, you'll keep your mouth shut about me and Joey."

"Ryan, wait." She leaped forward and caught him by the arm.

He stopped, not because of her hand's tight restraint but because of the note of panic in her voice. Slowly he faced her again.

"I can't lose both of you." Tears shimmered in the actress's eyes.

"I'm sorry." Ryan shrugged. "But you never had me."

Joey left Ryan's suite wearing her old jeans, stained T-shirt and leather jacket. It wasn't difficult for her to walk away from the designer clothes and expensive jewelry, but it was hard to leave the fantasy. The fictitious engagement, the unborn tribe of children and a Hollywood happily-ever-after all disappeared with the click of the door.

Good ol' reliable Peyton not only purchased her e-ticket, but she'd also wired money directly to the hotel's concierge. The money was much needed to pay for her taxi. Silent tears streaked down her face during the ride to the airport, but she refused to look back.

Joey had found, lived and lost love in a little over ten days. At least, she thought it was love—or was love what she had with Laurence? And what was the point of being the only one in love?

Ryan certainly never alluded to feeling the same way about her. Sure, he thought her beautiful or "perfect," and there was no denying he had a strong physical attraction to her. But love?

Joey thrust up her chin and decided she was doing the right thing. The only way to sort everything out was to step away from the situation. If after a period of time she felt the same way about Ryan, then…she would look him up.

She dried her face and refused to let another teardrop fall. It was time to rely on old-fashioned courage. Yet, as she said that to herself, a hope coursed through her heart, that Ryan would stop her from boarding her plane. Isn't that what always happened at the end of her sappy romance novels?

Ryan would find the letter she left and then race to the airport to stop her from making the biggest mistake of her life. It would be because he loved her—hopelessly so. Joey shook her head and laughed at herself, and then all too soon Milan Malpensa Airport came into view.

"If it was meant to be, he'll come."

* * *

"Lucy, I'm home." Ryan crept through the door with a wide smile and a bundle of roses and was a little stunned to find the suite as dark as a tomb. "Joey?" He reached for the main switch and clicked on the lights.

He called her name again and closed the door behind him. The place remained deathly silent as he removed his coat and then moved farther into the room. He glanced at his watch and thought surely Joey hadn't retired for the night at nine o'clock.

"Sorry I missed dinner," he called out, hoping to appease her if in fact she was somewhere in the suite sulking. "Taping ran a little late mainly because I'm working with an actress who thinks it's cute not to memorize her lines." He chuckled at his own joke.

He moved from the formal dining room to the corner living room but there was still no Joey. His frown deepened as he waltzed from room to room. Did she go to dinner without him?

Ryan turned to walk out of the main bedroom Joey used when his eyes landed on one of the pillows. He strolled across the room. When he recognized the ring nestled in the center of the pillow, his chest tightened. Once he arrived at the bed, he struggled with himself to pick up the heavy gem and the sealed envelope with his name written in Joey's loopy penmanship.

If nothing, Ryan was a realist, and everything about this small scene screamed *bad news!*

He drew a deep breath and contemplated whether to make himself a drink first. After a moment he rationalized it was best to get the whole thing over with.

Dear Ryan,

I can never repay you for all you've done for me
in the short time we've known each other. The last
few days especially have been wonderful and I
dare say you've come very close to winning your
bet. Maybe I'm a sore loser for leaving now, but
I need to save myself from myself. I don't know.
I'm starting to believe there is something wrong
with being in love with love. For one thing, you
begin to see it in everyone and everything until it's
all consuming. Pretending with you was nice and
easy, but in the end it will only hurt. I wish you
luck on your new film and I hope you'll think of
me from time to time…especially whenever
you're in a men's room.

Best of love,

Joseph H. Adams.

"Joseph?" Ryan stalled at the name. All along he'd
assumed Joey was short for Joanne or Josephine—but
Joseph? Just as quickly, his mind whizzed back to the
screenwriter who had written his dream project. "It
couldn't be."

A buzz at the door drew Ryan from his private
thoughts. He tossed the roses onto the bed, pocketed the
diamond ring and letter and rushed to answer the door.
Though he knew Joey had a key to the suite, it didn't stop
him from hoping it was her at the door. Her with woeful
eyes, admitting that she'd made a mistake in leaving.

Instead it was Zach.

Ryan's face collapsed in disappointment.

"Who loves ya, baby?" Zach grinned from ear to

ear and then rushed on into the apartment without an invitation.

"Zach, this isn't a good time."

"I'm not going to take much of you and your little lady's time." He glanced around, but made no further comment to Joey's absence. "Guess what."

"Skip to the chase and just tell me." Ryan grabbed his coat. "I have to get to the airport."

"I got your financing," Zach declared triumphantly, and then belatedly caught what his friend had said. "Why are you going to the airport?"

Ryan raced out of the suite. "I'll have to tell you on the way."

Minutes later Ryan and Zach climbed into the limo.

"To the airport," Ryan ordered.

The driver glanced back at him through the rearview mirror. "Which one?"

Ryan blinked and then made an educated guess that *Joseph* would fly out the same airport they'd arrived in last week. "Linate International."

Joey stalled at her gate until the last possible second. She tried to tell herself she wasn't really waiting for Ryan to appear out of nowhere and plead for her not to board the plane, but she knew it was a lie.

"We're about to shut the doors," the agent gently told her as if she sensed Joey's whole sad life story.

Joey nodded and expelled a long breath. From here on out she was going to stop reading those damn romance novels. Handing over her ticket, she scanned the crowded airport and swallowed an enormous lump of disappointment.

Maybe Ryan hadn't found the letter yet, she reasoned. Maybe she should have placed it on his box of cigars. Or maybe this whole thing was just a fling for him.

He had pretty much said as much. She was just someone to end his little dry spell.

"How do I always get myself into these things?"

With a heavy heart Joey boarded the plane and searched for her seat. Once again she'd booked into first class—or what P.J. had always called the first crash.

"Well, well," a familiar voice floated out to her. "This must be my lucky day."

Joey glanced up and was stunned to see her ex-almost-fiancé sitting next to her seat.

"I don't know about you," Laurence said, "but this must be fate."

Chapter 26

Six Months Later

Ryan arrived home and said nothing to the driver as he stepped out of the vehicle and into the chilly night. Tired, he exhaled gloomily as he stared at his sprawling mansion and wondered for the umpteenth time why he needed such a large place.

The answer once again came in a rush: in his line of work it was more important to appear successful than to actually be successful. Lucky for him he was both.

As he'd requested, no employees greeted him as he strolled through the door. As usual, the house's silence was deafening and the cold…humbling.

In the foyer, two sets of arched staircases ascended to the second level of the house. Ryan bounded up the right side, taking two steps at a time. He peeled out of the suit that he would undoubtedly never wear again and headed straight for the shower.

He paid no heed to how hot the water turned or how much the large bathroom filled with thick clouds of steam. His tangled thoughts focused on one thing and one thing only: Ms. Joseph H. Adams. He'd hoped that time and distance would weaken the memories and salve the pain.

He was wrong.

As it turned out, he remembered everything about the elusive beauty, and it seemed as if nothing would mend his broken heart. Not work, not alcohol, not other women—though he tried. The results: his... little problem returned.

Too bad women couldn't suffer the same ailment. However, he did pray Joey suffered with chronic headaches and a nonexistent libido whenever a man touched her. It was only fair.

Hours after *La Bella Vida* finished filming, Ryan hopped the first plane back to L.A. He wanted to return sooner, track Joey down and drag her back to Milan— but Zach all but pounded reason into his hard head. He was in the middle of a fifty-million-dollar production and no doubt the investors and producers would skin him alive literally if he walked off set.

However, now that he knew Joey was Joseph, and the writer of his dream script, it took no time at all to contact her agent and obtain Joey's address and phone number. The problem was getting her to call him back.

He was still waiting.

Shortly before being boiled alive, Ryan stepped out of the shower and toweled off. When he opened the door to the adjoining bedroom, a billow of steam preceded him.

His mind wrapped around all the things he could do to win Joey—all the things he could do to prove he wasn't with her just to win a bet or that he thought of her as a notch on a bedpost.

He'd sent flowers, jewelry and even a car—but everything was refused and sent back. When each gift returned, Ryan's desperation grew. Somewhere along the way when he wasn't looking Joey Adams stole the one thing he'd spent a lifetime guarding: his heart.

Somehow, some way, he had to get her back—her and their future eight children.

"Joey turned down two million dollars?" Sheldon thundered, above baby number five's cranky wails. "Is she crazy or something?"

"I'm going to give her the benefit of the doubt and say the 'or something.'" Michael rolled her eyes while her hairdresser finished pinning the French roll in her hair. "Let's not forget all the media hoopla she endured when she returned from Italy. Everyone wanting to know the 4-1-1 on her and Donovan."

"Don't you hate it when celebrities complain?" Sheldon chuckled. "I still say she should take the money. She's been at this screenwriting thing forever and a day and finally a studio wants to buy a script and she turns it down? It doesn't make sense."

Baby number five screamed.

"Shh, child. Shh." Sheldon unceremoniously whipped out a breast and proceeded to breastfeed.

"Geez. Will it kill you to warn someone before you

do that?" Frankie frowned as she eased into the chair in between Sheldon and Michael.

"What? Breastfeeding is natural."

"So is doing a number one and number two and I don't want you doing those in front of me, either," Frankie snapped.

"What the heck is the matter with you?" Sheldon asked.

"This damn wedding." Frankie tossed down her tube of mascara. "I can't believe you two are okay with this."

The hotel room's door opened and Peyton rushed through, carrying her pale-blue bridesmaid dress. "Sorry I'm late."

"Don't be sorry, we've only been here a few minutes ourselves. Sheldon dragged all five of the rug rats with her," Frankie griped.

"Of course I brought them. Ashley is the flower girl," Sheldon defended. "You're just mad that George isn't coming."

"Of course he's not coming," Michael said. She closed her eyes and allowed the makeup artist to brush on heavy strokes of blue eye shadow. "He didn't come to my wedding, either."

"Or mine," Peyton added.

"Hell, I don't think he came to mine, either," Sheldon said.

"No one went to your wedding—you eloped. Remember? You two pulled a Janet Jackson and didn't tell anyone you were married for a full year."

Sheldon shrugged. "Daddy would have killed us."

"He should have. You were seventeen," Michael huffed.

"Say what you want. We're *still* married."

Peyton and Frankie watched to see if Michael would explode at the reference to her pending divorce.

However, Michael smiled, though tightly, and said, "When you have a point, you have a point."

"Are you going to move back to San Jose?" Peyton asked, settling into her own chair to wait her turn with the hairdresser.

"I'm already packed. Of course I worry about Joey."

Peyton perked. "Hey, did you guys hear about the—"

"Two million dollars," Michael, Frankie and Sheldon said in unison.

"Yeah. We heard," Michael said.

"You know she's not taking the money because it's Ryan Donovan's production company. She thinks this is his way of buying his way back into her life."

"Hell, for that kind of money, he can have my spot," Sheldon said.

"Hear, hear," the sisters agreed.

A nervous Lincoln picked up his brother-in-law, Flex, from the airport. He'd put a lot of planning into today, and Peyton had wasted no time or breath in telling him when her brother picked up on what Linc was doing, he was going to flip.

"Are you sure this is a good idea?" Ronald asked for the tenth time today. "This could be seen as an ambush."

"Nah, nah," Linc waved him off with a nonchalance he didn't feel. "Flex will love you…I mean, he's going to like meeting with you."

"Yeah, but he's just coming into town for a family wedding. It might not be a good time—"

"Will you trust me on this?" Linc smiled, mostly because he was certain that he'd found the right man...partner...person for his lonely brother-in-law. He glanced over at his selection and supposed that another man would find the tall, lean brother attractive. He certainly thought Ron's affluent position, as vice president of Silicon Valley Bank, was a major plus, and if things worked out would be a great reason for Flex to move back to California.

Linc agreed with the Adams sisters. It was just too hard keeping tabs on him in another state.

"Linc, over here!" Flex shouted above the crowd.

Lincoln perked up and made another glance over at Ronald. Sighting his unkempt collar, Linc reached over to straighten it. "Remember, you're just a friend of the family invited to the wedding," he coached.

"I got it. I got it." Ronald laughed. "Now, stop it, you're making me nervous."

"Right. Right." Linc exhaled and turned toward the baggage claim. "Show time."

"She turned down the money?" Ryan paced the study, shaking his head. "Does she have a better offer?"

Zach stretched back in Ryan's leather armchair. "I don't think so. If you ask me, she's trying to prove a point."

"What point?" Ryan exploded exasperated.

"That's she not interested in your money, the flowers, the jewelry or the car. Of course, if you feel you must give someone a Mercedes—*Columpie un amor pequeño, mi manera.*"

"What's with the Spanish?"

"Well, since *Nation's* isn't for sale, Universal has a Spanish thriller they want you to look at."

"What am I—the United Nations of filmmaking?"

"I'm just saying that it's a good script. The writer was listed as a co-writer of *Candyland*—"

"Say no more. My answer is no." Ryan selected a new cigar from his desk. "I want Joey's script. Offer her another five hundred thousand."

"She's not going to take it," Zach said matter-of-factly. "She thinks you're buying the script as a way to get back with her."

"Did you tell her I've been trying to get this script green-lighted for six years?"

"Yep." Zach crossed his legs at the ankles. "And she didn't believe me."

"This is insane," Ryan huffed, lighting up. "I'm offering her way more than market price for a noncredited screenwriter," he ranted.

"I wonder," Zach said thoughtfully.

"What?"

He shrugged. "I'm just wondering if you know yourself whether you're upset about this on a professional...or personal level."

"It's both," Guadalupe answered, marching through the study's doorway. "If you ask me, you went about this all wrong," she fussed.

Ryan rolled his eyes. "So now everyone wants to give me pointers on my love life?"

"Someone needs to," Guadalupe sassed. "You think just because I don't live in some big mansion or make insane amount of money play-acting in front of a camera that I don't know matters of the heart?"

The two men looked at each other and came to the quiet understanding not to argue.

"Sure you can razzle-dazzle a woman with flashy things, but to capture a woman's heart cost nothing and yet everything at the same time."

Ryan stared at her, waiting for more, but when Guadalupe seemed finished on the subject, he jumped in. "Well…I guess that clears that up." He popped his cigar back into his mouth.

"You no understand, do you?" She jabbed a fist into her thick waist.

Once again, Ryan glanced to Zach but only received a blank stare.

She rolled her eyes. *"Jesús, me da fuerza."*

Zach chuckled.

"What is the one thing you value more than anything?" Guadalupe crossed over to his desk and then jabbed at his chest. "What is the one thing you spend your whole life protecting?"

Ryan was slowly catching on.

"Your heart," she answered her own question. "Anything you can buy with your money means nothing…because it comes easy to you. Understand? A woman who wants to plant roots and bear children will want something from you that no other woman has. And that is your heart. You give her that and she will make you the happiest man in the world."

Her words left Ryan speechless.

"In that case, I think you better hurry," Zach said, his face reddening. "There's something I forgot to tell you."

Chapter 27

"You set me up on a blind date at a family wedding?" Flex hissed to Linc as they entered the hotel suite to don their tuxedos. "I thought we've been over this. I want the family to butt out of my love life."

"What's the big deal?" Linc shrugged. "You didn't have a date."

"That's not the point," Flex snapped, punching his arms through the sleeves of his starched shirt. "Do you have any idea how many blind dates my sisters have set me up for?"

"C'mon. Ronald is—"

"One hundred and twelve," Flex said with irritation twitching in his jaw. "Should I tell you how many of them were successful?"

"But Ronald is—"

"One hundred and twelve."

"Okay, okay." Linc tossed up his hands. "So you've had a bad run. It doesn't mean you should toss in the towel."

Flex shook his head and fumbled with his tie. "You're as bad as they are."

"And you're just being difficult." Lincoln wrestled with his tie. "I'm trying to do something nice for you."

"Who asked you to?"

"C'mon, man. You saved my life once, remember? Not to mention you really helped me win Peyton—"

"That doesn't count. I was tricked into coaching you in winning P.J.'s hand."

"The point is, I want to return the favor. And though I don't know anything about man-to-man or gay dating, I do know Ronald is a very nice man with your sense of humor and it doesn't hurt that he has a great job. I assume those attributes are important across the board."

Flex grunted.

Linc took Flex's response or lack of one as a sign of a weakening defense. "He's a football fanatic and has an amazing car collection."

Flex was silent for a moment, and then, "Who is his favorite team?"

"Carolina Panthers."

Flex's eyebrows leaped upward while his lips compressed into a straight line.

Lincoln wasn't fooled. The panthers were Flex's favorite team as well. Encouraged, he shamelessly threw out more bait. "You know, Ronald invited Peyton and me over for dinner after my last art show. I tell you, the man should open his own restaurant."

"He can cook?"

"More like a culinary genius." Lincoln hid his smile as he turned and retrieved his tux jacket.

Flex cleared his throat. "Well, I guess since he's already here it would be rude not to, you know, talk to him."

"Yeah. That's all I'm saying. Talk to him," Linc encouraged.

Flex nodded and then suddenly his expression sobered. "This doesn't mean you're off the hook." He wagged a finger. "This thing can and probably will be the one hundred and thirteenth disappointment."

"See. You're going into this with the wrong attitude." Lincoln strolled over and swung his arm around Flex's shoulders. "Trust me on this."

Flex groaned just as the suite's door opened and a grinning Marlin strolled inside. "So, is everyone ready for the wedding of the year?"

Joey stared at her reflection in the mirror and hardly recognized the woman in the glass. The same was true for the past six months. However, it didn't stop her from hoping to snatch glimpses of her former self from time to time; yet, so far no such luck.

A knock rapped on the bathroom door, and Peyton's voice filtered through the wooden partition.

"Joey, are you all right?"

"Yeah. I'll be right out." She held her breath and waited to see if her lie would be successful.

The band of silence stretched tautly and threatened to break, but then Peyton's weary exhalation also seeped through the door followed by the sound of her slight footfalls padding away.

Joey's eyes returned to the woman in the mirror. She

was so tired of her family's constant inquiries and over-bearing "good intentions" that she could scream. Weddings were supposed to be happy and that was what she was determined to be. She forced on a smile, but a fine film of tears glossed her eyes from the effort.

"Goddamn it, Joey." She dropped her head and closed her eyes. A few tears were caught in the web of her eyelashes. "It's been six months. Get over it."

Her heart squeezed in answer to her request; however, her head swore it wouldn't allow her to ever make another fool out of them. It was bad enough that she had galloped across the globe after one man; she wasn't going to do the same thing for someone who thought there was a price tag on her heart.

Another knock sounded on the door; this time the voice belonged to Michael. "Joey, it's time to go down-stairs."

Joey snatched a blue Kleenex from its box on the counter and blotted her eyes.

"Joey," Michael's voice softened. "Are you ready?"

Drawing a breath, Joey pressed a hand down her dress. "As ready as I'm ever going to be." She turned and headed out of the bathroom.

Ryan made the drive from Los Angeles to San Jose in a little over three hours in his Porsche Carrera GT. Of course, it also included four speeding tickets, but he would deal with that at another time. Right now he was in a race to reach the Fairmont Hotel in the heart of San Jose.

However, he had no clue as to what he was going to do once he reached the place. Was he going to burst into the wedding on his hands and knees or was he simply showing up enough to jar Joey to her senses?

When Zach revealed Joey had turned down their last offer and then casually mentioned she had a wedding to get to by three o'clock, Ryan barked and nearly planted his fist in the middle of his friend's jaw. But he didn't have to glance at his watch to know that he didn't have time to kill his friend. He would do that later if he didn't reach the wedding in time.

He didn't have to question who Joey was marrying. The answer was obvious: Dr. Laurence Benson, asshole surgeon to the stars. Ryan's hands tightened around the steering wheel. Just the thought of what the former love-birds had been doing for the past six months while he was lovesick and impotent skyrocketed his blood pressure.

Then quite suddenly a memory played in Ryan's head. A memory of his flight to Italy:

"So it was love at first sight with you and Larry?" Ryan inquired, not bothering to veil his sarcasm.

"Not exactly," Joey plunged ahead, either ignoring or not picking up on his tone. "The stars were just lined up correctly. I'm the right age, he meets all my qualifications—"

"What?"

Joey blinked. "What, what?"

"Whatever happened to flowery prose or poetry? Things like 'I knew we were meant for each other the moment his hand touched mine' or 'the first time we kissed a bolt of lightning shattered my world and I knew I could never live without him?' Isn't that the kind of crap women eat up?"

"Sure—in books and movies—which I love. But in real life, you need a little more science and a check list."

His frustration mounted as he struggled to keep up with the conversation. "What's so scientific about the stars being aligned?"

"I don't know. My psychic can explain things a little better than I can. I know what you're thinking." Joey smiled. "I'm not crazy. Well, maybe crazy in love." She giggled.

Ryan rolled his eyes.

"Look, love is worth fighting for and that's all I'm doing."

Ryan chuckled under his breath at life's irony. He'd made fun of her desperation and now he was hoping his own would save him.

A hundred and fifty family and friends gathered inside San Jose's Fairmont Hotel to witness the marriage of yet another Adams. The colors were red for passion and pink for beauty. Nearly everyone buzzed with excitement and surprise.

Everyone except the immediate family.

Invitations went out one week and the wedding was set for seven days later. The rumor mill spun madly with suspicions of pregnancy—so everyone waited with heightened anticipation for the first glimpse of the bride's belly.

A hurried wedding planner sprinted down the aisle and signaled everyone to take their seats. A moment later the wedding march cued up and the first set of bridesmaids and groomsmen paced down the narrow aisle.

Genuine and plastic smiles blended and hung from the lips of everyone in attendance, but there was no mistaking the subtle gasp that rippled through the crowd when the bride stepped into view. Though a glorious vision in white, all eyes were drawn like magnets to the unmistakable second-trimester belly of the bride.

Chapter 28

Ryan was certain that if he didn't make it in time to stop the wedding, he was either going to have a stroke or a heart attack. Damn Laurence Benson, damn Zachary and damn *La Bella Vida*. He should have chased after Joey when she left Milan. He should have dropped to his knees and declared his love or have done anything to win her back. Anything was better than nothing.

He took a right onto South Market Street, and the Fairmont Hotel filled his vision. "Please don't let it be too late. Please don't let me be too late."

Tires peeled and squealed as he whipped into the parking lot. His heart still racked his chest as he leaped out of his car and raced into the large, spacious hotel with his feeble prayer still on his lips. "Please don't let it be too late."

* * *

Heart hammering, Joey glanced over at the groom and gave him a shaky smile. She could hardly believe this day had arrived, and couldn't believe further still that they were going to go through with it. She turned her head slightly and caught her sisters' wide, beaming smiles and knew that they were thinking the same thing.

Her heart skipped and suddenly her train of thoughts skipped the tracks. This was a mistake. Everything was happening too fast. When she realized that the groom was speaking, she cleared her head and tried to concentrate on what was being said.

"I love you," he said with twinkling eyes. "Today is a very special day. Long ago you were just a dream and a prayer. And this day is like a dream come true. For today, you as my joy become my crown."

Joey smiled and allowed a small tear to streak down her cheek.

"Thank you for being what you are to me," the groom continued. "With our future as bright as the sun, I will care for you, honor and protect you. I will lay down my life for you, my friend and my love. Today, I give to you…me."

More tears raced down Joey's face while a lump wedged its way into her throat.

All eyes locked onto the bride, and just as her painted red lips opened to speak her vows, the doors to the ceremony crashed open.

"Stop the wedding!"

A percussion of gasps rippled through the room.

Joey's head whipped around at the familiar voice

while her eyes grew wide as silver dollars. "What on earth," she whispered.

"I'm in love with this woman," Ryan declared to the stunned crowd. "And I believe that she's in love with me, too." Ryan strained to see Joey's face hidden behind the white veil as he strolled down the aisle. But his eyes strayed and landed on Joey's very pregnant belly. Hope and dread pulsed through his body. Was he the father? Would she allow him to love the child even if he wasn't? No one else and nothing else mattered to him.

"I'm miserable without you," he admitted. "I can't sleep, think or eat. You're all I want and need. You don't love him." Ryan shook his head, hoping to convince her. "I know we only knew each other for a brief moment, but in that moment, you've changed my life."

Joey couldn't breathe, and her tears nearly rendered her blind.

"I want you beside me—every day for the rest of my life. I want to wake up to your smile and fall asleep listening to your breathing. I want us to have those eight children with at least one girl with your smile." Ryan's own tears pooled behind a dam and threatened to overflow and spill down his face. "Tell me I haven't lost you. Tell me that it's not too late."

Slowly the bride lifted her veil and met Ryan's stunned gaze. "But…I don't even know you."

Ryan blinked and blinked again. But no matter how hard he tried, he couldn't get his eyes to reconstruct the beautiful woman's face to look like Joey.

"Ryan," Joey hissed from behind the bride.

His eyes shifted and immediately recognized the bridesmaid as Joey.

"What are you doing here?" she hissed again.

"What?"

"Did I miss something?" the groom, an older gentleman with Joey's eyes, questioned, and glanced between his bride and Ryan. "Who is this guy?"

"Sorry, Dad," Joey apologized. She stepped around the bride and grabbed Ryan by the arm. "I think he's here for me." She tugged Ryan as she rushed up the aisle, her face scorched with embarrassment. To add to her humiliation, Ryan started laughing in her wake.

"Do you know what you just did?" Joey barked, rounding on him after the doors slammed behind their departure and they stood alone in the reception room. "My family is never going to let me live this down."

With her eyes lit with anger and her body coiled tight for an attack, Ryan snatched her up against him and smothered her fire with a long kiss. In it he poured everything he had into her: his hopes, his dreams and his passion.

In no time at all, her body went limp and her mouth grew as hungry as his own. Her long slender arms twined around his neck and pulled him closer.

She tasted better, smelled sweeter and felt softer than he remembered. He squeezed her tight, and vowed to never let her go.

But time slipped away from them, and before either of them had a chance to think, the doors slammed open again and another train, formerly known as the wedding party, crashed into the smooching couple.

Ryan didn't know what was happening. All he could see was the bride's big belly, plus someone was crushing his legs. "Get off," he croaked. "Get off."

A minute later, though it felt much longer, the pressure on his spinal cord loosened and the sound of laughter jingled in his ears. By the time he was pried up off the floor, laughter chorused through the reception room.

The bride and groom waved to the crowd to show that they were all right and then mingled with their guests while their laughter and merriment continued.

Ryan would have joined in if two mountains, one with Joey's eyes, hadn't hauled him up and held him suspended in the air.

"You have a lot of explaining to do," the first mountain said.

"Linc, Flex, put him down." Joey dusted off her dress.

"He nearly ruined Dad's wedding," Flex complained, his grip tightening on Ryan's arm.

Easy intimidation wasn't normally in Ryan's repertoire, but he had a sinking suspicion the two men could actually do some damage to him if given the green light.

"Let him go. I love him," Joey admitted.

Ryan blinked in surprise, and judging by Joey's expression, she was equally surprised by her words.

A small ring of people closed in on them.

"Did we hear you right?" A bevy of beauties, all with Joey's eyes, nose and voluptuous lips inquired in unison.

Ryan's gaze locked with Joey's; his heartbeat somehow seemed suspended in time.

Joey lifted her chin, whether in defiance or feigned bravado, he wasn't sure. "Well, I guess that sort of depends."

"On?" Ryan along with the circle of women and two mountains inquired simultaneously.

"On whether or not I'm just another head game...or whether he just wants me because I'm something he doesn't have...or he thinks buying my screenplay for some outrageous price is going to win me over...or whether he really, truly wants eight children."

"Oh, dear Lord, she's been hanging around Sheldon too long," Michael said with a roll of her eyes.

"You're not a game to me," Ryan confessed, his heart warmed with a ray of hope. "And of course I want you. I wanted you from the first time I saw you crawl into the men's bathroom."

"Do what?" the small circle thundered.

Ryan ignored them. "I'll always want you—whether you wear my ring or not. And truth of the matter is I've been trying to get your screenplay green-lighted for six years. I had no idea your real name was Joseph until you wrote me that letter in Milan. And I want as many children as you'll give me."

The mountains set him down.

Everyone's eyes shifted to Joey with anxious anticipation.

"Well, well," Marlin said, shouldering his way into the circle, his smile wide and his eyes dancing with amusement. "Has this young man won my daughter's hand yet or is he going to make another try at my new wife?"

Joey's chin lifted another notch. "I don't know. It depends on if he brought a ring."

Ryan reached into his pocket. "You're in luck. I brought two."

The women gasped.

"You can either have your original ring—" he pried open one velvet box "—or you can have this one." He opened a second box and revealed an antique silver band with small diamond baguettes. "It was my grandmother's. Once upon a time she was the most important woman in my life. She sheltered me from a lot of storms between my father and mother. I know that she would want you to have it."

Fat tears welled up and rolled down Joey's face. "It's beautiful."

Encouraged, Ryan lowered onto one knee. "Joseph Henry Adams, will you do me the honor of becoming my wife?"

"Yes," she answered quickly and raced to him.

"It looks like there's going to be another wedding!" Marlin shouted. He turned and motioned his new bride into the family fold. She went to him gladly as the entire wedding party erupted in good cheer.

Joey and Ryan sealed their love with a kiss. Each knew that they had finally found what they'd been looking for all their lives.

"By the way," Joey said. "I'll take the two million for the screenplay."

Ryan burst out laughing. "You got yourself a deal."

Author's Note

Hmmm. Interesting. It looks like fickle Joey has finally found her soul mate. Even Dad is jumping back into the love business…with another Adams in the oven. Do you think it will be another girl? It even looks like there's hope for Flex and Ronald. At least, I hope so. A hundred and thirteen blind dates. Yikes!! But what about Michael and Frankie? Both seem a little disillusioned by love. However, if you ask me, there are a few surprises just around the corner….